DOCTOR WHO

IN AN EXCITING ADVENTURE
WITH THE DALEKS

D1497725

THE CHANGING FACE OF DOCTOR WHO
The cover illustration and others contained within
this book portray the first DOCTOR WHO whose
physical appearance was later transformed when he
discarded his worn-out body in favour of a new one.

Also available from BBC Books:

DOCTOR WHO AND THE CRUSADERS
David Whitaker

DOCTOR WHO AND THE CYBERMEN
Gerry Davis

DOCTOR WHO AND THE ABOMINABLE SNOWMEN
Terrance Dicks

DOCTOR WHO AND THE AUTON INVASION
Terrance Dicks

DOCTOR WHO AND THE CAVE MONSTERS
Malcolm Hulke

DOCTOR WHO

IN AN EXCITING ADVENTURE
WITH THE DALEKS

Based on the BBC television serial *The Daleks* by
Terry Nation by arrangement with the BBC

DAVID WHITAKER

Introduction by
NEIL GAIMAN

Illustrated by
Arnold Schwartzman

BOOKS

3 5 7 9 10 8 6 4 2

Published in 2011 by BBC Books, an imprint of Ebury Publishing
A Random House Group Company
First published in 1964 by Frederick Muller Ltd

The Random House Group Limited Reg. No. 954009

Addresses for companies within the Random House Group can be found at
www.randomhouse.co.uk

A CIP catalogue record for this book is available from the British Library.

ISBN 978 1 849 90195 6

MIX
Paper from
responsible sources
FSC® C016897

The Random House Group Limited supports The Forest Stewardship Council
(FSC®), the leading international forest certification organisation. Our books
carrying the FSC label are printed on FSC® certified paper. FSC is the only
forest certification scheme endorsed by the leading environmental organisations,
including Greenpeace. Our paper procurement policy can be found at
www.randomhouse.co.uk/environment

Commissioning editor: Albert DePetrillo
Editorial manager: Nicholas Payne
Series consultant: Justin Richards
Project editor: Steve Tribe
Cover design: Lee Binding © Woodlands Books Ltd, 2011
Cover illustration: Chris Achilleos
Production: Rebecca Jones

Printed and bound by CPI Group (UK) Ltd, Croydon, CR0 4YY

To buy books by your favourite authors and register for offers,
visit www.randomhouse.co.uk

Contents

Introduction by Neil Gaiman   vii

The Changing Face of Doctor Who   xi

1. A Meeting on the Common   1

2. Prisoners in Space   17

3. The Dead Planet   35

4. The Power of the Daleks   50

5. Escape into Danger   66

6. The Will to Survive   83

7. The Lake of Mutations   98

8. The Last Despairing Try   121

9. The End of the Power   137

10. A New Life   160

About the Authors   163

Between the Lines   167

Neil Gaiman
IN AN EXCITING INTRODUCTION WITH THE DALEKS

It was another world, in those days.

Understand me, and try and picture it: we had no video cassettes, no DVDs, no on-demand anything, no YouTube, no iPlayer. There was no way of seeing an episode of a show you had missed. There was no way of re-experiencing a television show you had enjoyed.

Well, *almost* no way. There were records you could listen to, big vinyl scratchable things, with the songs from films you'd liked, or even with old radio shows on them. These were not entirely satisfactory. There were also, and these were much better, books.

Books let you go back through the story as many times as you wanted. They were always waiting for you, doors into worlds you wanted to revisit. They were 360-degree, full-sensory recreations, extrapolations or interpretations of television and film you had loved.

There are still 'novelisations' of films and TV shows, but in the old days, back when this book was written, books really were the only way back to something you had loved, the only way to visit a story you had missed.

And unless you were watching television in early 1964, you missed Doctor Who's first encounter with the Daleks…

I was three years old in 1964. I'd only just turned three. My birthday was in November. I was at Mrs Pepper's Nursery School in Purbrook in Hampshire. John F. Kennedy had been shot a few months ago, but nobody told me about it. Back in those days children got free milk at school. It came in bottles that held a third of a pint. We drank our milk with a straw in our mid-morning break.

One break-time, when they had finished their milk, a few of the other boys did something odd. They bent the straws over, when they had finished drinking their milk, so the ends of the straws resembled eye-stalks, and they moved the bottles around the table, making threatening noises and saying, 'I-Am-A-Dalek!' Which was how I discovered *Doctor Who*.

My television-watching at home at that age was tightly controlled by my mother and limited to the amiable puppet vapidities of the BBC's Children's Hour: *Andy Pandy* and *The Flowerpot Men* and the like, in strange stories I expected I would understand when I was an adult, because they made no sense then. My grandparents, I am glad to say, were less concerned that television be used in a Positive and Educational way, so it was at their house in Southsea that I watched *Doctor Who* early on Saturday evenings, and when I got scared I watched it from behind the sofa, because the monsters couldn't get you if you were behind the sofa.

Each episode was precious. It could not be revisited.

Which is why, by the time I was six and living in Sussex, and in control of the buttons on the TV, and when I watched *Doctor Who* from anywhere in the room I wanted to, and when the behinds of sofas were places I almost never watched television from any longer, my most precious possessions were a couple of *Doctor Who* annuals, a copy of another annual called *Dalek World*, and a paperback copy of the book that you are holding.

I did not know who David Whitaker was, not then. I knew that he had novelised Terry Nation's Dalek story, though. I knew that he had taken us into the TARDIS, and I made a point of searching for his name whenever I visited bookshops or libraries.

That book was my talisman. It was where I learned how it started. The cover was a moody painting of the TARDIS with the First Doctor in front of it. It's old and battered now, from so much reading, but I have it still.

(The book I loved was almost but not quite, this book. It was the Armada paperback, with different illustrations and a different cover. The human-armed dragon monster on the back cover looked sort of funny to me then and looks even funnier now, but you can't see it, so you'll just have to take my word for it.)

I was surprised, years later, to learn that on the original TV series it didn't begin in the fog, that Ian Chesterton wasn't an unemployed job-hunting scientist but was a teacher. Surely this was how it began, on the heath, in a world that had faded to white.

The book was also my way of getting further into the TARDIS than we seemed to be permitted to do on the TV. I loved the Food Machine that made things that looked like Mars Bars and tasted like bacon and eggs. (I tried to sneak that into the *Doctor Who* episode I wrote, and it was there for a couple of drafts.) I loved looking at this place through Ian's eyes.

Watching the DVDs of 'An Unearthly Child' and 'The Daleks' in later years was a wonderful thing, but still…

I'm glad that there were books. The magic of pure fiction is this: that you are there. And I got to look through Ian's eyes as he travelled in the TARDIS; I visited Skaro, and I met the gentle Thals; I was never as scared of the Daleks in the books as I was scared by them on the television, but in the book I got to see inside the Dalek casing to the creature within and it gave me the creeps in a way that fiction had never done before. The television never managed that, to show me the unimaginable, until Rob Shearman's story 'Dalek' almost forty years later.

I read the rest of the *Doctor Who* books, the ones that were available anyway, in hardback at my local library. One of them was even by David Whitaker.

There are many joys in this book. I liked Susan and Ian and Barbara. I really liked the portrait of the conniving, brilliant, arrogant Doctor. I was not sure that I really liked *him*; I definitely didn't trust him. A man who could break his own mercury fluid link might do anything.

No, Susan's grandfather was not ever quite my Doctor. I remember the initial shock of learning that Patrick Troughton had replaced William Hartnell, that there was now a new Doctor (but he was still the same Doctor – a 'Phoenix in the Tardis' as one of the articles in the *Doctor Who Annual* described him), and then the discovery that he was still the Doctor – and that, strangely, he was my Doctor. I knew I'd be safe with him. He was just as alien, but he was reassuring in a way that the prickly First Doctor had never been.

But that never stopped me picking up this book, and it never stopped me loving it, looking for clues, wondering about the nature of the Doctor, of who he was, and where he and Susan came from, and why they had left…

And although some of those questions have been answered, I love the fact that, almost fifty years later, so many of them remain mysteries and secrets.

Now, read this book. Visit another world.

The Changing Face of Doctor Who

The First Doctor

This *Doctor Who* novel features the very first incarnation of the Doctor. When the Doctor was younger, he was an older man. It seems strange now, but when television audiences were first introduced to the Doctor, nothing was revealed about his origins and background. We knew only that together with his granddaughter, Susan, he has fled from his own planet in the TARDIS – which he cannot control. Every trip is a mystery and a surprise as the TARDIS could take him anywhere and anywhen.

Brilliant but crotchety, the First Doctor did not suffer fools gladly. He took his first companions – Barbara and Ian – with him out of necessity rather than choice. It was more of a kidnapping than a privilege. Over time, and perhaps because of his contact with human beings, the Doctor mellowed and became less irascible. But his brilliance and his passion for justice remained undiminished...

Susan

Susan is the Doctor's granddaughter. Although she attends school under the name of Susan Foreman (she is renamed Susan English in this novelisation – see 'A Note on the Text'), that is probably not her name any more than it is the Doctor's.

Susan looks and behaves like a typical 15-year-old girl. It is at her insistence that she attends Coal Hill School, and it is here that her strange breadth of knowledge in some areas, and total lack of it in others, is noticed by her teachers, who decide to investigate...

Ian Chesterton

In the television series, Ian Chesterton is a science teacher at Coal Hill School. While his occupation is altered in this novelisation, his character remains very much the same.

As a science teacher, Ian Chesterton believes when he can see the proof. This makes him initially a sceptic when he finds himself inside the TARDIS, asked to believe that it can travel in time and space. But once he has proof, once he has seen and convinced himself, he proves to be the most practical of the travellers.

Ian is not short of common sense, or of bravery and courage. He eventually wins the Doctor's respect to the point where the old man treats him almost as an equal, almost as a friend. Before long he is revelling in his new-found life – and is even knighted by King Richard the Lionheart. But he never loses sight of the fact that he wants more than anything else to get home.

Barbara Wright

History teacher at Coal Hill School, Barbara Wright accepts the apparent impossibilities of travel through time and space more readily than Ian. She is practical, realistic, but also more instinctive, and once she realises the truth she accepts it entirely.

This combination of intuition and practicality make Barbara the ideal mediator in the TARDIS. From the start it is Barbara who manages to smooth the way between the Doctor and Ian. But when she is convinced of something, she is more than capable of standing up for it. She enjoys her adventures in space and time – especially those that take her back into Earth's history, but like Ian she never loses her determination to get home.

CHAPTER ONE

A Meeting on the Common

I stopped the car at last and let the fog close in around me. I knew I was somewhere on Barnes Common and I had a suspicious idea it was the most deserted part as well. A warm fire and the supper my landlady would have waiting for me seemed as far away as New Zealand. I wondered how long it would take me to walk home to Paddington and the possible answer didn't do anything to cheer me up. A fitting end to an impossible day, I thought savagely.

For a start, before breakfast, I'd torn my best sports jacket on a loose screw on the door of my room. It didn't help that I'd been putting off tightening it for weeks so I had nobody to blame but myself. Then later, after I'd driven all the way to Reigate for a job I was after as Assistant Research Scientist at Donneby's, the big rocket component firm, I found that a nephew of one of the directors had got the post and I'd made the journey for nothing. Now the fog and the prospects of a long, weary walk. I looked at my watch, delaying the decision as long as possible. Nearly nine o'clock.

Just as the second hand completed its minute, I heard the sound of running footsteps. Probably somebody as lost as I was, I told myself, welcome for a delay from the final decision to begin walking. Suddenly, into the pallid glow of my head lights, a girl appeared. She stopped and I saw her hands moving slightly, and I could see her mouth opening to speak. I tore open the door and ran to her, catching her before she fell to the road.

1

She hadn't completely fainted and I could just make out the name she was saying – Susan – as I lifted her up and put her in the front seat, then her head rolled back on the seat-rest and she passed out altogether. She was in her early twenties, I guessed, and she had one of those deceptive sort of faces; attractive, yet with strong character. Her clothes were covered in mud and her stockings hung in ribbons about her legs. There was a big rip in the jacket of her suit on her shoulder and I could see the blood spreading over the material. I opened the bonnet and dipped my handkerchief in the radiator. This put an end to any idea of walking, I told myself. The cut on her shoulder didn't look too good and might even need some stitches in it. I went back to her, wringing out the handkerchief, wondering why she didn't have a handbag. Had somebody attacked her and stolen it? The obvious solution didn't occur to me.

She began to move her head a little as I bathed her forehead. Her lips quivered slightly.

'Susan… Susan…'

All I could think about was how strange it was that she should want to tell me her name and I suppose I was so preoccupied with this line of thought that it was almost startling when she opened her eyes and looked at me. There was a pause of a second or two and then I laid the handkerchief against her forehead.

'Rest quietly for a minute. You'll be all right.'

'Susan…'

'Yes, I know. You started to tell me your name before—'

She shook her head and I rescued the handkerchief and started to refold it.

'No, Susan is on the road,' she said, 'she was in the car with me.'

'I'll go and have a look in a moment.'

'No, now. Please!'

I heard the urgency in her voice. I nodded.

'All right. Is it straight ahead?'

'I'll come with you. I must. She's hurt.'

'What happened?' The answer came to me almost as soon as I asked. 'Car crash?'

'Yes. Thank heavens you pulled up. You'd have driven right into it.' She started to get out of the car.

'You've hurt your shoulder, you know.'

'It's all right.' I helped her out, pretending I hadn't noticed the agony on her face as she moved her injured shoulder.

'You'd better show me. But say if you don't feel up to it.'

We began to walk along the road and we had taken only a few steps before the fog swallowed up the headlights of my car and the fog pressed in around us.

I said, 'How badly hurt is she?'

'I don't know. There was a lot of blood on her face. It was a big lorry. An army one, I think.'

We groped our way forward, inching our way, but still I nearly tripped over the shattered wing of the lorry that had been wrenched away from the main bodywork. I guided the girl around it and broken glass began to crunch under our feet. It was a strange, eerie sound in the silence of the night. The outline of the lorry appeared and we circled round it cautiously. It was lying on one side and sprawled half in and half out of one of the driving cabin windows was the upper half of an army corporal. I climbed up as far as I could on the twisted metal and it looked as if the man had been hurled sideways at the moment of impact, the glass of the window shattering but holding him from being thrown out into the roadway. I stared at him for a second or two and then stepped back on to the road.

'Is he all right? Hurt badly, or what?'

I looked at her, wondering what state she was in to hear

what I had to say. The pause seemed to be sufficient for she turned her head and peered through the eddying mist at the body.

'He's dead.'

'I'm afraid so.'

The fog was beginning to line the back of my throat and, for the first time, I became aware of the strong smell of petrol. One of the lorry's headlights still glared out into the night and I thought the less chance the petrol had the better. I felt a sudden anxiety that there would be a short circuit and the whole wreckage would explode in our faces. I climbed up again.

'I'll have to turn the lights off but don't move for a moment. We'll never find each other again.'

It was an unpleasant business. I had to engineer the dead body back into the cabin before I could wrench open the door and then scramble over to reach the light switch. The smell of petrol was stronger than ever inside the cabin and it was becoming more and more difficult to breathe, but I managed to reach the switch at last and my world plunged into impenetrable blackness.

Fear had always been a thing that I'd read about, a condition of the mind that was a total mystery to me because I'd never experienced it. I suppose every person has the odd moment of fright now and again, like the second between tripping and hitting the ground; but I had never felt fear so deeply before. It flooded through me, damping down my mind from logic or reasoned action and making the cold sweat stand out on my forehead.

Someone, somewhere, struck a match. I heard it quite clearly, the long scrape of the sulphur head against the short strip of sandpaper, the brittle flare of ignition. I banged my head as I scrabbled to get out and away from the lorry and the petrol all around me, hearing a ripping of cloth as my coat

4

caught in a piece of protruding metal. I felt the girl's hand on my arm steadying me as I raced to get down.

'Did you hear it?' I said breathlessly. She stared at me. 'Somebody's here. Striking matches! The petrol…'

I swallowed and tried to get control of myself.

'You must have imagined it,' she said quietly.

'No, I didn't. I heard it quite clearly. On the other side of the lorry.'

We stood there shouting for a while, straining to hear some reply or movement. There was nothing but the cold, deadly silence.

She said, 'Perhaps it's Susan.'

She started to lead me away from the wreckage and up the road and I had a feeling I'd disappointed her in some way. I apologized for frightening her and she turned and looked at me steadily.

'I should be the one to apologize for involving you in all this.' As we groped our way forward, I thought about what she'd said and it seemed to me that there was something else in her words other than a reference to the crash.

'I couldn't very well sit in my car when you were fainting all over the bonnet, could I?'

'I didn't mean that.'

I didn't go on asking questions but I knew I'd been right. There was something else behind the accident itself. It was the appearance of her car through the wreaths of mist that put an end to conversation. Its nose was buried into a tree and the familiar sound of broken glass began to crunch under our shoes as we picked our way around it.

'Can you possibly get the boot open? There's a torch in there.'

I turned the handle and wrestled with the bent metal for a few moments. Eventually it gave and I was able to force it upwards. I felt around and found the torch, hoping it was in working order. The light flashed on and I heard the girl give a little exclamation of relief. I picked it out carefully, not bothering to close the lid of the boot. Her car was a complete write-off anyway.

'You'd better show me where she is.'

'I managed to get her out of the car to the side of the road.'

She led me round and then stopped so sharply that I almost cannoned into her.

'Susan,' she said quietly, and then louder, 'Susan!'

I flashed the torch about. Apart from the ever-present broken glass, there wasn't a sign of anyone.

'Perhaps it *was* her. The match-striker, I mean.'

She shook her head. 'She had a terrible cut on her forehead. Quite a lot of blood. It was on her face and her pullover. I'm sure she was unconscious.'

'But no stranger's going to just come along and move her,' I argued. 'Move her where, anyway? We're in the middle of Barnes Common.'

'She told me she lives here. Very near here.' If she felt me looking at her curiously she gave no sign. 'I was just pulling up when the lorry skidded across the road and hit us.'

'But how could she live here? The nearest house must be over a mile. It must be.'

'I know. We – argued about it. She hadn't wanted me to drive her home at all but I simply wouldn't let her travel alone in this weather. I insisted.'

'And she told you to drive her to Barnes Common?'

The girl nodded. I thought for a moment.

'When I told you about hearing the match striking you said then you thought it might be Susan. Now you tell me that she was definitely unconscious and couldn't have moved.'

'Oh, I don't know,' and I heard the weariness in her voice. 'It couldn't have been the Doctor. I know this part of the Common. There isn't a house near here.'

'What doctor?'

'Her grandfather's a doctor.'

I leaned against her car.

'I wish you wouldn't let things out a bit at a time,' I said as carefully as I could and suppressing the irritation I felt. I knew she must be somewhere near breaking point.

'If her grandfather's a doctor, then he must have moved her. It was probably he who struck the match too. The thing is, what we're to do next. There's no doubt that he'll come back here as soon as he's settled Susan in bed and start looking for you.'

She said, 'There's every doubt in the world.'

After the silence while I digested what she'd said, I must have moved my hand in exasperation. The light from the torch picked up the shine of something other than glass about five yards away. I crossed and picked up a small brass ornament with a broken piece of black tape threaded through the hole at one end. I showed it to the girl.

'It was Susan's. She wore it round her neck.' Her voice was flat and emotionless and I suddenly began to feel angry.

'It's no good standing about here talking!' She looked at me sharply and I suppose I had spoken rather loudly. I shrugged.

'You can't blame me for losing my temper. You keep on hinting at things, as if this weren't just a terrible road accident but something more. A girl who lives in the middle of a Common; too unconscious to move and disappears as soon as your back's turned. This doctor, the grandfather. Why all the mystery?'

'I can't tell you much because I don't know very much.'

'But this *is* just a road accident, isn't it? What else is there, for heaven's sake!'

7

'There's her disappearance to worry about.'

In the silence, I offered her a cigarette. She refused and I lit one for myself. In the glow of my lighter flame I saw the tears on her cheeks. The only logical thing I could think of was that she was suffering from shock but even as I toyed with that idea I realized it didn't seem to fit. There was nothing nervous or hysterical about her at all, no signs of extreme panic. One or two curious things had happened and she had made a couple of strange comments. I decided the exchange of cigarette smoke for fog didn't help and flicked the cigarette away. It gleamed briefly for a moment and disappeared, and as I turned to start asking the girl some questions my whole body suddenly froze into a complete stillness.

The footsteps I heard were cautious ones. I could almost imagine the owner picking his way carefully and not just because of the poor visibility either. This sort of walking was deliberately quiet. I felt the girl's fingers touch and then hold my arm. We both pressed ourselves back against the wreckage of the car and waited. I switched the torch off.

The dim outline of a man became clearer. He was wearing a cloak and under his fur hat I could see his silver hair, surprisingly very long on the back of his neck and touching the collar of his cloak. His head was bent down, peering at the ground and in his hand he held a lighted match. He stopped suddenly, so near to us that I could have taken three steps and stood next to him. I saw him bend down on one knee and pick up something from the pavement. It was my cigarette.

All my concentration was directed towards the match he was holding. The strength of its light never altered and the quality of it was far whiter than any match I'd ever seen before. The other thing that puzzled me was that it didn't seem to be burning any lower.

Slowly he turned his head and the girl's hand gripped even

8

harder on my arm. He saw me first and then he looked at the girl beside me.

'What are you doing here?'

It was such an extraordinary question in the circumstances that I nearly burst out laughing. He got up and stepped over to us, holding the match higher in his hand. I felt it was up to me to say something.

'A girl's been hurt. We were looking for her.' He nodded slowly.

'A tragic business. The soldier in the lorry has been killed. You've been hurt, too, young lady, by the look of you. You should be in bed.'

'Not until I've found Susan,' she said quietly, and the old man gave her a sharp, almost startled look.

I couldn't stop myself any longer.

'What is that match thing? It never seems to burn down.'

'Just a little invention of mine,' he said easily and turned his attention to my companion. 'What did you say happened to the girl?'

'She was hurt. I told you. I left her here on the pavement and went to get help. When we came back she'd gone.'

'Made her own way home, perhaps?'

'That isn't very likely, is it?' I said. He waved a hand in the air, a gesture of bewilderment.

'The young are so thoughtless.' I saw his eyes glinting with malicious amusement. 'Perhaps one of her family found her and took her home.'

I didn't understand why he should be amused and, what was worse, his whole attitude was adding another layer of mystery to the business.

'Perhaps you'd like to help us look for her,' I said coldly. 'Better still, take us to your house. We ought to ring for the police. All this wreckage on the road can cause another accident.'

'I wouldn't worry about the girl. I'm sure she's in safe hands. As for a telephone, I'm afraid my little nest doesn't possess such a thing.'

I tried to muster up all my patience. 'Then perhaps you could offer a hot drink and a chair for this lady. She's been hurt too, as you said yourself.'

He looked at her and clicked his tongue in sympathy. It was the most insincere sound I've ever heard in my life.

'The trouble is, I've lost my key. That's what I was looking for.' He shot a look at me of such intense directness that I blinked. 'You haven't seen it, have you? Picked it up, perhaps? It's brass. There may even be a piece of black tape attached to it.'

I pulled it out of my pocket. 'Yes, I picked this up.' His hand stretched out for it but I closed my hand around it and looked at the girl.

'But you said it belonged to Susan.' She nodded. I turned my attention back to the old man again. 'Apparently, she wore it around her neck. Now I'll tell you what I think. You've found the girl, haven't you? And now for some reason or other you want this. Never mind about anybody else being hurt or injured or anything.'

'Are you trying to give me a lecture on human behaviour, young man?' he said sharply. 'I won't tolerate anything of that kind. You possess something that belongs to somebody else. Please give it to me.'

'Yes, it does belong to someone else. And that someone doesn't happen to be you. Have you taken that young girl somewhere?'

I spoke the last three words into the fog for the old man turned quickly and was swallowed up. I could hear his running footsteps. I glanced at the girl and saw the indecision in her eyes, but I wasn't in the mood to leave it all to speculation. I took her hand firmly and she came with me without protest as we ran up the road after him. After a few seconds I couldn't hear his footsteps any more and slowed down. I flashed the torch about me and made out the square shape of what seemed to be a hut set back from the road on the Common itself. I walked towards it and then both the girl and I stopped and stared at a police telephone box.

'Now we're all right,' I muttered. The trouble was, I couldn't get the door open. I banged my fist against the double doors in frustration.

'But these things ought to open,' I said angrily. 'What are they here for but to help people in trouble.'

She said, 'What's it doing on the Common?'

I turned the light of the torch full on her face.

'I don't care about disappearing girls, strange old men *or* where the police choose to put their telephone boxes.' I took a deep breath, struggling to control myself, and managed to speak more reasonably. 'All I want is to finish with this business and get home.'

'Yes, I'm sorry.'

I shut up for a minute, ashamed of losing my temper with her. It wasn't her fault after all. In the pause, I heard a twig crack and I wheeled round, shining the torch in an arc. The old man stepped forward.

'I see you've found the police box, young man,' he said cheerfully.

I stared at him for a few seconds, collecting my thoughts.

'And if I could open it, I'd have a squad car round here and let them get some sense out of you.'

'Now, now, you mustn't lose control of yourself, you know. Locked, is it? How extraordinary.'

His whole attitude was so friendly that I doubted my own

memory of our first meeting. He stepped over and looked at the girl beside me carefully.

'This appalling weather isn't helping you at all. And there's blood on your jacket. Most distressing. You have a car, of course?'

I nodded, completely speechless at his change of manner. He rubbed his chin reflectively.

'What I suggest is this. You take the young lady back to your car. Try and make her comfortable. Then come back here with a crowbar or a jemmy or something and we'll try and force open this door. Isn't that the wisest thing to do?'

'All right,' I said reluctantly and turned to the girl. 'If you agree?' She nodded. The old man rubbed his hands together and beamed at us.

'Capital! Order and method, young man, there's nothing like it. Off you go now and don't be long with that jemmy, will you?'

I turned to go, helping the girl as she nearly stumbled over the uneven ground. I couldn't get rid of my suspicions of him and the more I thought about it, this sudden geniality made it worse. I stopped and felt the girl's eyes on me. She must have seen something in my face, a growing conviction that we were being fooled. She turned and looked back. I heard her catch her breath and I turned as well.

The old man was holding up his lighted match, which still hadn't burned any lower down the stem, and his other hand held a little sliver of metal which glittered. He put the metal into the lock and the door started to swing open. At the same moment he turned and looked at us. It was a look of malevolent cunning and triumph suddenly mixed with concern that he had been caught out. I ran back towards him and caught him by the shoulder. The doors continued to open slowly and a fierce, glowing radiance began to emanate from behind them. I leapt at the old man and we fell heavily to the ground. I could hear him snarling at me to let him go and not meddle in his affairs, but the words didn't make too much impression on me because all I could think about was that whatever it might look like from the outside, I knew perfectly well that this was no ordinary police box on Barnes Common. Out of the corner of my eye I saw the girl go past me towards the opening doors.

'Stop her! Don't go through the doors,' the old man shouted desperately.

I heard another voice calling. 'Grandfather,' it said. The girl stopped at the open doors.

'Susan! Susan, are you in there?' She turned and looked back at me and I held the old man quiet for a moment. 'He must have put her in here.' She went through the doors.

The old man sobbed with anger and tore himself away from me, and then as we both scrambled to our feet the scream echoed out from the telephone box and stopped us both. He was the first to move but I gave him a sharp push and he staggered away and fell again on one knee. I raced over to the box and ran through the doors.

The light closed around me and I screwed my eyes up in agony and threw my hands up to my face. Almost at once, I tripped over something and fell headlong forward, hitting my head with a sickening crash on the floor. Weary and half dazed, remaining conscious only because of the memory of that pitiful scream, I tried to lift myself up on my knees and gradually opened my eyes, hoping the blinding light might have lessened. What I saw gave me a clarity greater than a bucket of freezing water tipped all over me.

The terrible glare had diminished down to the ordinary electric power of a well-lit room, although I could see no evidence of any bulbs or fittings anywhere. The first real shock was the immense size of the room around me. This is a police

13

telephone box, I kept repeating to myself. Just a small box big enough to hold two or at the most three standing people. I relaxed on my haunches and stared around and above me. I was in a room about twenty feet in height and with the breadth and width of a middle-sized restaurant. I calculated there would be room for at least fifty tables. In the centre was a six-sided control panel, each of the six working tops covered with different-coloured handles and switches, dials and buttons. In the centre of this panel was a round column of glass from which came a pulsating glow. The walls were broken by serried ranks of raised circles, this pattern itself being interrupted by banks of machines containing bulbs that flickered on and off. In one corner I spotted a row of at least twenty tape-recording spools spinning round furiously, while beneath them a similar number of barometric needles zig-zagged uneven courses across moving drums of paper. To make this nightmare even more unbelievable, dotted about the room were what looked to me like excellent copies of antique furniture. Here was a magnificent Chippendale, there a Sheraton chair. A most elegant Ormulu clock stood on a carved stand and beside it was another stand of marble upon which was a bust of Napoleon.

I hit my head, I told myself. I've fallen in the telephone box and I'm imagining it all. I tried closing my eyes and opening them again but it didn't make any difference except that I became aware of the figure of a young girl staring at me. Her eyes were very dark and she looked frightened. I noticed that her clothes were normal enough, dark ski trousers and boots and a cherry-red sweater, although she was wearing a most extraordinary scarf tied closely around her forehead. It had thick red and yellow stripes on it and made her look like a pirate. I tried to smile, although the pain was back in my head where I'd hit it on the floor.

'Now I know this is a dream,' I said weakly. I heard a

14

buzzing sound behind me.

'Close the doors, Susan.' It was the old man's voice. I saw the young girl move to the control panel obediently and turn one of the switches. The buzzing increased and I swung myself round on the floor. The double doors closed behind the old man. In front of him I saw the body of the girl I had met in the fog. She was lying full length on the floor and one of her shoes had come off. The old man examined her briefly. The young girl who had answered to the name of Susan walked past me and knelt beside the body.

'Is Barbara all right?'

The old man shrugged.

'Fainted. Her pulse is steady. We must do something about that injury to her shoulder.'

'And who's that one?' That one was me. They both regarded me thoughtfully and then the girl went on, 'He wasn't with us in the car.'

'Your teacher met him on the road after the accident,' replied the old man. 'I'm extremely cross about this, Susan. You should never have let Miss Wright bring you out here.'

'I couldn't help it, Grandfather. She insisted.'

'Then you should have stayed the night at her flat. I'm sure she would have offered you a couch and a blanket and you know I wouldn't have worried about you.'

The girl said, 'But I would have worried about you.'

The old man walked over and stood in front of me.

'Well, now we have someone else to worry about.'

I felt consciousness slipping away from me. The bang on the head must have been worse than I thought. A black cloud was beginning to roll over my brain. My eyelids were as heavy as lead and my head started to fall. The old man bent down on one knee, put a hand under my chin and held my face. All the power was draining away from my arms and legs and I couldn't have lifted a finger to stop him, even if he'd started to hit me.

'He's going under. There's a bump the size of a golf ball on his head.'

The black cloud was blanketing down now and I had a terrible sensation of falling slowly into a bottomless well. I heard the old man speaking as if from a long way away.

'The point is, can I let you go now? I don't think I can. I'll just have to take you both with me.'

Then I blacked out completely.

CHAPTER TWO

Prisoners in Space

I was standing in a cylinder of metal and it was so hot I could feel the sweat dripping off my forehead and running down my face. It was absolutely black but somewhere above me a circular metal door was being opened. I saw a tiny pin-point of light and the vague shape of a person climbing down towards me. Somehow or other I knew the person was nervous.

'Don't drop the light,' I shouted, 'whatever you do, don't let go of it!'

I saw the light slip out of the person's hand and it plunged towards me. It got larger and larger until it filled the whole of the cylinder above me. It was a blinding light that hurt the back of my eyes and I knew it was going to smash into my skull.

I woke up and the light was the soft light of a room. The sweat became little drops of water escaping from a cloth that was pressed against my forehead. The girl called Susan was sitting on the bed beside me, smiling with relief.

'I knew you'd be all right. Barbara was very worried about you.'

Barbara. The girl in the fog. The old man. Memory flooded back and at the same time I felt a throbbing pain on the left side of my forehead. The girl squeezed out the cloth and laid it across my forehead.

'My name's Susan. We might as well get to know each other since we're to be together.'

'Are you my guard?'

'You're free to come and go as you please – inside *Tardis*,' she replied seriously.

'Thanks very much. What's *Tardis*?'

Susan waved her hand above vaguely. 'This is. I made up the name from the initials.' She changed the cloth over my head, waiting for me to ask her what initials, but I didn't. She told me anyway. I knew she was going to.

'"Time And Relative Dimensions In Space".'

She began to take off the cap of a small, orange-coloured tube. She squeezed a little of the contents, a thick brown paste, on to her index finger and rubbed it on the sore place on my head.

'This stings a little but it'll get rid of the bump in half an hour.'

It stung more than a little and I could feel my eyes watering, but at least the throbbing stopped. I was determined to be as nonchalant as I could until I was absolutely sure I was awake. I looked around me. The room was small but the walls were identical to the other one I'd seen when I'd run through the doors, with raised circles on the walls and no evidence of lighting although it was as clear as day. The bed I was on had a soft, foam rubber mattress and was shaped rather like a deck-chair, except that it was bent and raised under my knees. I looked at the girl again and found she was watching me.

'Grandfather will explain everything to you,' she said. 'I'd better tell him you're awake.'

She got up and moved to the doorway and the glass door slid open into the wall as she approached. I put my hands together and gripped them as hard as I could because it had been a police telephone box I'd run into and I didn't like what was happening. She turned and looked back at me.

'I hope you didn't get that job you were after with Donneby's.' I just stared at her for a moment or so and then shook my head. She looked genuinely relieved as if I'd cleared her conscience about something and went out. I took the cloth from my head and used it to dab the tears in my eyes. The ointment had begun to stop stinging now, but I was suddenly aware of a tiredness in all my muscles. I also realized that I wasn't wearing my overcoat or the jacket of my suit and somebody had taken my shoes off, I tried to get off the bed but my body didn't want to move. I sank back, thinking I'd have another try in a few seconds.

The old man came into the room, followed by Susan and the girl she'd called Barbara, who looked very pale but completely under control. She came straight over to me and sat on the bed and took one of my hands.

'How are you now?'

'A bit weak. What's happening here?'

Her eyes looked away, as if she had something to be guilty about. I saw Susan open two of the circles in the wall and take out three stools. The old man sat on one and Susan the other, but Barbara stayed where she was.

'The Doctor will tell you everything,' she said.

I turned my eyes and met his. Without his cape or fur hat, he still clung to the costume of another age. A tapered black jacket, the edges bound with black silk and the trousers Edwardian, narrow and patterned in black and white check. He was even wearing spats and a cravat with a plain pearl tie-pin. His long silver hair and the pince-nez hanging around his neck by a piece of thin satin tape completed the picture. He had every right to wear eccentric clothes if he liked, I thought, but it simply didn't fit with the ultra modern surroundings.

He fitted the glasses firmly on his nose and pulled out a wallet and some other papers from his pocket. I was determined not to speak until he did, even though he had taken them from my jacket without asking. I wasn't confident enough of my muscles yet.

'Ian Chesterton.' He darted a look at me over the top of

his glasses and then started sorting through the papers and letters. 'You're a schoolmaster with a degree in science. You don't like being a teacher much, I gather. Well, I suppose that shows ambition although a certain lack of early purpose.' He sniffed as if he didn't approve of the way I was running my life. I couldn't feel any fury or anger, yet I wasn't indifferent either.

Suddenly he smiled at me. There are some men of sixty who smile and merely appear to be genial elderly men, and there are others who become younger. If I was right in my guess of his age, the smile made him shed about twenty years. I was surprised how much better I felt when he was friendly and realized that it quietened the awful anxiety and the suspicions about my sanity. You can't experience too many things outside normal explanation without thinking you're either dreaming or insane.

'Chesterton, you have certain qualities I admire,' he said cheerfully. 'Perhaps my hasty decision will prove to be a blessing. For one thing, you do not ask a lot of stupid, ridiculous questions. You're content to wait until you hear the facts. It is also extremely fortunate that you're a student of science because it suggests a rational mind. Have you any idea where you are?'

'No idea at all, and I'd rather you didn't praise me about my lack of curiosity yet. I have rather a lot of questions.' He waved his hand airily.

'Well, that's natural enough young man. I must take you slowly, though, step by step.' He crossed his legs and tapped his glasses on his chin for a moment. 'Let me put to you a hypothetical situation. Let us say you are a spy in a foreign country. You have a secret hiding-place where you keep all sorts of things that are dangerous for even the most ordinary people to know about. One day your hiding-place is discovered, quite by accident, by an unsuspecting member of the public. What do you do?'

I felt Barbara's hand tighten on mine for a second.

'Be patient,' she said quietly.

'Oh, it's all right. This is all leading somewhere, I can see that.' I turned back to the Doctor, as she had called him. 'I'd have to give up the hiding-place.'

'Because you'd be afraid of publicity.'

I agreed.

'Of course, if your hiding-place was an aeronautical machine…'

'Aeroplane, Grandfather,' interrupted Susan, and he looked at her sharply, getting the silent apology he demanded. The old man turned his attention back to me again.

'Now, where was I? Ah, yes. Your hiding-place is an – aeroplane. It is discovered. Now what do you do?'

'Destroy it?'

'And lose your escape route? Surely not. Wouldn't you fly it away?'

I agreed patiently that I would, if it were possible.

'Good. We make progress. Now these people – innocent members of the public who have stumbled across your hiding-place?'

I knew the answer to that one because the analogy was childishly simple, even if the reasons behind it were not. 'I might have to take them with me,' I said slowly. The Doctor rubbed his hands together.

'Excellent, Chesterton! These innocent passers-by might spread the news abroad of your presence, mightn't they? Yes, you might have to decide to take them with you, however inconvenient it might be to you.'

Barbara said: 'Or to them.'

After the silence, I said, 'So the sum total of all that is to tell me that you have some sort of flying machine or aeroplane and you've taken us with you.'

21

He nodded vigorously. 'You've grasped the essentials, Chesterton. Of course, my granddaughter and I are not spies, as you may well imagine.'

'Of course not.' I thought I might as well let this go on as long as possible, until I felt stronger.

'However, we do have the strongest possible reason for not wishing anyone in your world to know of our existence.'

'In my world?'

He looked at Susan briefly. Now we get to the biggest lie of all, I thought. Here it comes.

'My granddaughter and I are from another world. You and your companion are at present inside my Ship, the *Tardis*, which is able to cross the barriers of the fourth and fifth dimensions: Time and Space.'

I didn't say a word. Barbara's hand held on to mine as if she were petrified of the old man and I didn't blame her. It wasn't funny to be so close to a raving lunatic. After the pause, he went on:

'The young lady next to you, who I can introduce to you as Miss Barbara Wright, was engaged by me as a special tutor for Susan. I wanted Susan to become as well versed as possible with the culture and manners of England in the twentieth century. Furthermore, Susan professed a curious preference for the liberties extended to young people of this day and age.'

The Doctor stood up slowly and looked down at me, fingering his glasses thoughtfully.

'We're wanderers, Chesterton, Susan and I. Cut off from our own planet and separated from it by a million, million years of your time.'

He really believes all this, I told myself. There was a genuine sadness in his eyes as he looked away from me.

'There'll come a day when we return.'

Susan got up from her stool and put her arms around him.

They mean all this, I told myself. They aren't acting it, they're really serious.

'One day we will, Grandfather.' He patted her head affectionately then stepped away and looked at Barbara and me.

'You blundered into my Ship and I had to decide what to do quickly.'

'I did everything I could to persuade him to let you both go,' said Susan, and I felt the girl beside me catch her breath slightly. Don't tell me she believes what they're saying, I thought. The Doctor was speaking again.

'But I decided against it. I have operated the *Tardis* and we have left Earth. There is just one more thing I would say at this time.'

I raised my eyebrows deliberately.

'Oh, only one?'

The Doctor stared at me for a moment.

'Even on your planet you have a rule, I believe, that says there can only be one Captain to a ship. As Susan has told you, I have no doubt, you are at liberty to come and go as you please within the *Tardis*, but you must follow my orders without question at all times.'

My body was still weak but I felt like testing it so I swung my legs off the bed and stood up, with Barbara beside me. Maybe I looked rocky because I felt her hand under my arm. I was glad of it because I found my legs were about as reliable as rubber bands.

I said, 'Now I'll tell you what I think. It was that blinding light that fooled me when I ran through the doors. I suppose there was some sort of trap-door there and we both fell through it. This is some cellar or underground cave that you've discovered and you've dressed it up with all sorts of gadgets to fit your story.'

I had to sit down again; it wasn't any good fooling myself. What surprised me more than anything was that the girl beside me was shaking her head slowly at me. You're wrong, her eyes were saying. I supported myself on the bed as best I could and ignored her.

'I want you to ring for a taxi to take us both home. I can't drive like this.' A sudden thought occurred to me and I looked at the old man in alarm. 'You have warned the police about all that wreckage on the road, haven't you?'

'Chesterton, you must believe me. Forget about your planet. We're already in the next Universe but one.'

He turned on his heel and walked out. Susan started to follow him and then looked back as she reached the doorway.

'It's all true, Mr Chesterton. Every word of it.'

'It's a lot of ridiculous nonsense,' I said angrily. At last I felt anger rushing through me. Susan glanced at Barbara desperately.

'Tell him. Make him understand. It mustn't be too great a shock.' She turned and followed her grandfather and the glass door slid into place behind her.

Barbara walked away slightly and sat down on one of the stools, her head turned away from me.

I said: 'I'll be all right if you can give me five minutes. Then we'll get out of this mad-house.'

'I'm afraid we won't.'

'Wouldn't you like me to take you out to dinner somewhere? I think we both deserve it.'

She still turned away from me, silent and uncommunicative. I put a hand up to my forehead and the bump had completely gone. Whatever the ointment was that the girl had smeared on, it was certainly very quick. I tested my legs again and felt stronger. I stood up and there wasn't any dizziness any more. I tried a few steps, keeping near the bed just in case, but I didn't have any more trouble. Suddenly I found that Barbara was watching me.

I crossed over to her and sat down on the stool next to her.

'For some reason or other you believe the old man, don't you?'

'There isn't any reason behind this,' she said slowly. 'This is something that's happened beyond our powers of reason. We just have to accept it.'

'I don't have to accept anything. What's he done to you for heaven's sake? Listen, the girl's all right. Let's get out of this asylum and leave them to their own fantasies. It's only about a hundred yards down the road to my car. I can run you home.'

She shook her head slowly and turned her head away from me again. The old man has really convinced her, I thought. She got up from the stool and walked over to the glass door and looked through it. I noticed that it didn't slide open this time.

'I'd like to tell you how this all started. For me.' She turned and looked at me inquiringly.

'All right, if it will tell me why you automatically believe everything the old man tells you.'

She leaned against the glass door.

'I put an advertisement in one of the papers about four months ago – "Extra cramming in special subjects. Personal tuition. Prefer History or Geography but will generalize." You know the sort of thing. I was fed up being a secretary in an office and those were the subjects I knew well. I thought it might be the beginning of bigger things. I rather fancied the idea of running a school all of my own and I've done quite a lot of teaching anyway. Relief work and that sort of thing.' She smiled briefly. 'I only had one reply, asking me to ring a certain telephone number. I did and spoke to Susan. She told me her name was Susan English and that her grandfather, a doctor, wanted her to have a course of special studies in History. From ten until four every day except Saturdays and Sundays. I asked if I could meet her grandfather and discuss the eventual object of the classes – was she to try for one of the universities? Why she wasn't going to a finishing school? How much I was to be paid and so on. Susan told me I couldn't meet her grandfather because he was very busy on research but that the object was to have a working knowledge of general English History and that I was to be paid twenty pounds a week.'

I stared at her.

'I don't wonder you took her on.'

'Well, it wasn't only the money, although that was marvellous. I think I told Susan every week it was too much but she just laughed about it and said her grandfather was very rich.'

'What about her previous schooling?'

'Yes, I asked her about that. She just said she'd been travelling. In fact, she was pretty vague about every question I asked her.'

'Surely in four months you must have found out something definite?' I argued.

'Once in a while she'd let something slip out. She hadn't seen her mother and father for a long time; she'd never been to England before; little things like that. It never got anywhere because she simply turned the conversation away whenever I tried to follow something up.'

She moved away from the glass door and sat opposite to me on one of the stools. 'It was in the History itself where I learned most about her. She once wrote me a thirty-page essay on Robespierre, which even went into details about what walks he took and the measurements of some of his clothes. On the other hand, she made the most terrible mistakes.'

'Such as?'

'She thought Australia was in the Atlantic Ocean. Oh, a dozen and one things. She thought the Spanish Armada was a

26

castle. Some of them were so wrong they were laughable. And it wasn't a lack of attention or carelessness. She was really upset when she made a mistake. She started crying once when I was cross with her because she had written that Japan was a county in Scotland.'

I burst out laughing but Barbara didn't seem to share my amusement.

'I know it seems funny, but looked at in another way it's a little frightening don't you think?' I shrugged. 'Anyway,' she went on, 'I was determined to have a chat with this grandfather of hers. The last two or three weeks have been a succession of evasions and excuses. Then tonight there was fog and I insisted on driving her home. I practically forced her.'

There was silence for a moment or two while I considered everything she'd told me. I had to admit there were some strange things to explain away. None of it made me change my opinion that the old man was either very eccentric or a lunatic. I wasn't feeling too happy about the young girl called Susan either. I was just coming round to the belief that some straight talking was in order when the glass door slid open and Susan looked in.

'Grandfather says you can come out now. We'll be arriving soon.'

'And will it still be foggy on Barnes Common?'

She didn't smile. I had the uncanny feeling she thought *I* was the one who was insane.

'It's very kind of your grandfather to tell us when to come or go,' I said coldly. 'You might tell him we certainly are coming out. And furthermore,' I stood up and heard the anger sharpening my words, 'you can tell him I want those doors open and no more arguments.'

Susan turned and went out of the room again without saying a word and I turned to Barbara.

'You've told me a story that had some odd things about it. The whole evening has been peculiar. It's made you believe one thing and it's made me sure of another. Let's go and find out who's right and who's wrong.'

She nodded briefly and walked into the other room. I followed her and we walked through a short corridor that was made up entirely of tall, square pillars of coloured glass, the reds, blues and yellows alternately glowing and dying down. I thought about the old man's electricity bill and had to admit he'd gone to a lot of trouble and expense to bolster up his absurd story of travelling from another world. Then we turned into the first room I'd seen, the control room as the Doctor called it, and I saw him standing over the central panel, his hands darting from switch to lever to button, pressing some and turning off others. I began to feel a faint shivering in the floor beneath me

and the lowering decibels of an engine whine sounded in my ears. The Doctor looked up and beckoned us over to where he was standing.

'Stand near me,' he commanded, 'and look up at the scanner screen.'

'Never mind about any of that,' I said sharply. 'Open the doors and let us out.'

He leant on the panel and looked at me seriously.

'You disappoint me. I had the mistaken idea that you were intelligent. Or at least that you had some imagination.'

The shuddering started to increase in the floor and I could feel it tingling up through the bones of my legs.

'I don't know what you think you're doing but if you don't open the doors I'll kick them down,' I shouted. It wasn't anger or fear that made me shout at him. The engine noise was now filling the control room. It was rather like a dozen of those war-time sirens all running down and not quite together.

'You won't have to do any kicking,' he said, quite mildly I thought. 'I will open the doors in a moment and then you'll see for yourself.' He glanced at Susan. 'So dogmatic, my dear. They can't accept anything they can't explain.'

'She believes us, Grandfather.'

I looked at Barbara. She was staring up at the place the old man had told us both to watch, the scanner screen. I looked too. There was a kind of mist, rather like the fog on the picture, and I was sure we were looking out on to Barnes Common for a moment. Suddenly the floor gave a final shudder which made all of us stagger and Barbara clutched hold of my arm for support. The whine of the engines stopped suddenly and in dead silence I saw the screen clear. I felt the first real doubt since I'd run through the doors of the police box. I was looking at an extraordinary forest of white looking trees. The picture altered and gave a closer view of one of the trees. There were no leaves and it had a dead look about it.

'Not particularly inspiring,' murmured the Doctor, 'but not very dangerous either.'

'Where are we?' asked Barbara.

The Doctor shrugged. 'Very difficult to say. I do have what Susan is pleased to call a "yearometer". Unfortunately, on a previous expedition it was slightly damaged. I really must get around to seeing if I can't mend it.'

'But we're not… in England any more?' The old man looked at her in surprise.

'I thought I'd made that quite clear, Miss Wright. We have not only left England but we've left Earth. I shall have to sample the atmosphere outside and do various other little tests, but we'll know more in a few moments.'

'The temperature seems quite good,' Susan said.

I took three short steps and swung the Doctor round.

'Now listen, you! I'm fed up with all this game playing. If you don't open those doors, I swear to you I'll smash them down.'

He knocked my hands away sharply and it crossed my mind that he was surprisingly powerful for a man of his age and build. He stepped back and suddenly pointed a finger at me, his eyes gleaming with fury.

'You invaded my Ship! I didn't ask you in here, you assaulted me and forced your way in.' He dropped his hand and some of the fury died away in his eyes, to be replaced by a superciliousness that didn't do my temper any good at all.

'All that stupid, ridiculous mystery out on the road,' I stormed. 'Why didn't you tell us you were Susan's grandfather? Why lie about the key? Why run away? Of course we were worried because we didn't know who you were and Susan was missing, so don't start accusing people of forcing their way into your home when you know perfectly well there was an excellent

30

reason to do so.'

'Yes, well that's all fairly logical, as far as it goes. Concern and curiosity are valid feelings, but scepticism, my dear Chesterton' – and he was so superior I felt like kicking him – 'yes, scepticism is a failing in your world.'

'Then open the doors and let us take our feelings as far away from you as possible.'

There was a short pause, then the Doctor turned his head and looked at Barbara.

'I believe you have more of an open mind on the subject, Miss Wright.'

'It doesn't make sense to me,' she said, 'but, yes, I believe you.' I looked at her in astonishment.

'How can you accept any of it? Time and space travelling, people from another world – it's all absolute nonsense.' The Doctor gave a short, harsh little laugh and walked up to me and tapped me on the chest with his forefinger.

'I imagine this is the treatment Columbus received when he propounded his theory of your planet being circular.'

'For a space traveller you seem remarkably well informed about the history of Earth.'

'I have read a little,' he admitted, 'but I much prefer to experience history. The younger Columbus was a man of such obvious promise that I always regretted leaving him before he made his theories known.'

I looked at Barbara helplessly.

'You can't believe this man, you simply can't! At the very least, he's an eccentric…'

The Doctor brushed past me rudely. 'Open the doors, Susan,' he ordered. 'That's the only way to make this young fool realize.'

'But we haven't checked everything properly yet, Grandfather.'

'I don't care about that. I simply won't stand here and be subjected to insult from a young man whose intellect can't even stretch out to accept known and proved scientific fact. Open the doors!'

Susan turned a little black switch. The lights glowed all around us again and there was the sound of that buzzing noise I'd heard before, rather like a swarm of angry bees. The two great double doors began to swing open. The Doctor marched towards them and looked back as he paused before going out.

'You wanted to go out. Come along.'

I moved after him slowly, only just conscious that Barbara was walking beside me. The trouble was that I could see past the Doctor quite clearly and what I was looking at was what I had seen on the scanner screen. White, dead-looking trees, a kind of ashy soil, a cloudless sky. The heat fanned my face as I stopped at the doorway of the ship. I heard Barbara make a small sound in her throat beside me. Somebody touched me on the arm and handed me my shoes which I put on, only half aware that other hands were tying the laces. I heard Susan's voice telling me I ought not to walk about in stockinged feet, because there was no telling what the ground would be like. I didn't do any of the conventional things that one reads about, like pinching myself or rubbing my eyes. I just stood there and stared about me, a dead horror of total realization creeping through my body.

He *had* been telling the truth. Every word made sense to me because there wasn't any other way of explaining it. I wanted to run away, to hide, to scream out in absolute fear, but where could I go? What was the point of being afraid? I almost felt rather than saw the Doctor standing in front of me and the kindness in his eyes helped me back to a sort of reality.

'Chesterton,' he said gently, 'this is the hardest part of all for you. I know exactly what you're going through and it's no triumph for me to be right. I have transported us all away from your world and your Universe and we have landed on a new planet. Accept that because you must. Tears and anger will not take you back to Earth, so learn from this new experience and profit by it.'

I nodded dumbly and he patted my arm pleasantly enough. 'That's right, Chesterton. You'll soon get used to it.' He looked at Barbara.

'You're extraordinarily cool, my dear, but I sense the sadness about you. As I have just said to your companion, try to rise above what has happened to you. At first it may be horrifying to you to be wrenched away from what you know and love and trust. I understand that, but isn't there an enormous excitement in doing what none of your people has ever believed possible? It's not a form of mental torture but a privilege to step out on to new soil and see an alien sun wheeling above you in another sky.'

He stepped back, regarded us both with a slight smile, then turned and moved towards the nearest tree. Barbara and I stepped out of the Ship and Susan came behind us and closed the doors. Then she ran over to her Grandfather and I heard her thanking him for being so nice to us. I turned my head and looked at Barbara.

Her face was white but there wasn't a tear anywhere on her face or in her eyes and I thought her composure was one of the most admirable things I'd ever known. I thought of the rotten interview I'd had at Donneby's and my subsequent depression at failing to get a job I wanted so much. I thought of a ruined supper at my digs, the fog on the Common and tearing my best sports jacket in the morning. I suppose the triviality of that last memory made me smile slightly and suddenly I realized that Barbara was smiling back at me.

She said, 'We'd better keep up with the Doctor.'

I nodded and we started to walk over to him. The world, my world, and my life on it seemed already to be moving into the distance. I glanced over my shoulder and looked at the Doctor's Ship. Outwardly, just as it had been on the Common, it appeared to be a police telephone box, but I knew without any doubt at all that inside it the dimensions were different. Around me was a world that was new to me and might well be totally different from anything I had ever come up against before.

I didn't know whether I hated it or disliked it or what I felt yet. I only knew that the Doctor was right and that I had to accept it. Either that or go completely insane. Insanity would imply that everything around me was a stage setting of the mind, that I was hypnotized or drugged. Dreams and nightmares, I knew only too well, never sustain belief for very long and the more time I took to examine my surroundings and match them against my actions and sensations, the weaker the idea of fantasy became. I was certain I wasn't hypnotized, I was sure I had not been drugged and I was positive I wasn't dreaming.

I began to feel better. The Doctor had told me the wisest thing to do would be to open my mind and accept what had happened.

I did.

CHAPTER THREE

The Dead Planet

It was about twenty minutes later that I heard Barbara scream. We had penetrated quite deep into the forest of dead trees and then stopped for a breather. The Doctor decided to examine the soil and together he and I puzzled over its ashy texture. It was almost as if there had been a terrible fire in the forest at some time or another, yet this didn't match up with the trees. They simply crumbled away when you touched them. Susan and Barbara went off in different directions, having been told to keep within calling distance by the Doctor, and Susan returned carrying a most delicate and beautiful flower she'd found. It was crystallized, of course, and the slightest touch would shatter it to pieces. I was just taking it from her to examine it more closely when Barbara screamed and the flower disintegrated in my hands.

I ran towards the sound, the branches of trees cracking and powdering in clouds around me as I forced my way through. I found Barbara with her back pressed up against a tree, the knuckles of one hand pushed hard against her teeth. She was staring away from me into some bushes. I taught the glint of the eyes of some animal or other and stopped dead still.

'I just came around this tree and it was facing me,' she whispered. I kept my eyes on it but there wasn't a single movement. It was half hidden in some bushes but I could see the unnatural shine of two squat legs and the scales of its body gleamed dully in the speckled sunlight that shone through the trees above us. It was about the size of a small pig and eyes

sprang out of the monster's head on long stalks. I heard Susan and the Doctor crashing through the forest after us and when they came into view I motioned to them cautiously.

'Get ready to run.'

I eased Barbara away from the tree that was giving one or two ominous creaks anyway as the pressure of her body increased. I led her away slowly and still the animal didn't budge an inch.

Susan said, 'I think it's dead.'

'I wouldn't like to test that theory,' I replied grimly. I had just caught a glimpse of its mouth and the jaws looked as dangerous as a small crocodile, with sharp teeth jutting out hungrily.

'The eyes don't move at all,' murmured the Doctor. He bent down and picked up a twig and threw it at the animal and the protest died in my throat when it still didn't move a muscle.

I picked up a fallen branch carefully, feeling it beginning to crumble in my hands, and edged my way forward. I prodded with the stick into the bushes and there was a slight tinny sound as the stick broke over the animal's back.

'You were right, Susan, it is dead. Looks as if it's been petrified like everything else in the forest.'

The Doctor walked over and rapped his knuckles on the animal's scales. As he pushed the bushes away we had a full view of the thing. It had a tail at least twice as long as its body and sharp spikes ran from the head right down the spinal column to the tip of the tail.

'It isn't petrified,' said the Doctor. 'It's solidified. This is metal.'

Barbara had overcome her fear and she knelt down beside him. 'But that's impossible!'

'Why? Because you can't imagine an animal that might be made entirely of metal? I tell you this *is* a metal monster, or rather was. Held together by some inner magnetic force, I shouldn't wonder. It probably had the ability to attract its victims towards it, for quite clearly it fed upon metal as well.'

He stood up suddenly. 'Ashy soil. Crystallized flowers, dead trees and solidified metal. What does that suggest to you, Chesterton?'

'Heat, obviously. Concentrated heat and yet...' I stared at him. 'An atomic explosion of some sort.'

'Precisely. A gigantic one, too, and yet not an atomic or a hydrogen one as being experimented with on your planet. That would simply sweep everything away from the crust of this planet. Here, we have things in some sort of preservation.'

Susan said, 'There's a kind of path over here.'

The Doctor motioned us to follow her. 'I hope I haven't brought you to a dead planet, Chesterton,' he murmured glumly. His disappointment was so obvious I had to smile and

I looked across at Barbara on the other side of him.

'You don't imagine we'd rather have met a live one of those monsters, do you?'

'It would have been a good subject for study,' he muttered and I saw Barbara raise her eyes in mock surprise. Then Susan ran back towards us.

'There's a city!' she cried in excitement. 'I can see it where the forest ends.'

We ran after her and I found myself caught up with her excitement, as if finding a city was the discovery of the century. The Doctor hurried on ahead of me, his long white hair streaming out behind him, his arms working away at his sides and when we came up to where Susan was standing I noticed that he didn't seem to be out of breath at all. I only hoped that I'd be as fit as he was when I reached his age.

The forest did end, just as Susan said, and the little path broadened out into a clearing where the ashy soil was very loose and deep. Ahead of us, there was a long line of tall rocks and Susan was standing on a small boulder, shading her eyes against the sunlight and looking through a cleft just ahead of her. She turned back and watched us ploughing our way through the soil and laughed at us suddenly. I imagined from what Barbara had said that Susan was aged about fifteen but silhouetted there as she was, with her dark, short cut hair against the white rocks behind her, she looked like a young woman in her twenties, very attractive and vivacious. I wondered briefly what would happen when she met a man she wanted to marry and decided not to travel in the *Tardis* with her grandfather any longer. This opened up too many questions about what planet the Doctor and his granddaughter had come from originally and whether the people on it knew about such Earth-like customs as marriage. I put the questions aside for another time and helped Barbara climb up on the boulder and the four of us (for the Doctor had scrambled up beside Susan with remarkable agility) stared through the cleft in the rocks at the city.

It was about a mile away, I judged, and looked like a cluster of electrical gadgets. There were polished metal domes that shone in the sunlight, all sorts of tall, square shaped buildings and what I described to myself as electric pylon masts and radar scanners dotted liberally around the domes and buildings.

'Quite magnificent,' breathed the Doctor, and I had to agree. Whoever had designed it and whatever its purpose, there was an exact and beautiful symmetry about the construction and the lay-out.

Barbara said, 'Well, that doesn't seem to have been affected by the explosion or whatever it was that destroyed the forest.'

'Do you think anyone lives down there, Grandfather?'

The Doctor shook his head. 'I don't quite know why the city is still intact but I'm certain there was some sort of huge explosion in this area. People couldn't survive. Not,' he went on slowly, 'people as we know them, at any rate.'

I digested this. I'd seen for myself a creature made of metal in the forest. It seemed possible that there might be survivors of some sort living in the city. I was so busy with my thoughts that I only just caught the gist of what the Doctor was saying.

'I'm afraid I can't let you do that, Doctor,' I said slowly.

'That city, I repeat young man, is a subject for examination and I intend to make a survey of it.' I shook my head.

'Not without preparation. Not without discussion either. We don't know what's down there and it may be dangerous.'

'I intend to go alone,' he replied tartly, 'so you needn't be afraid.'

'But I *am* afraid, Doctor. You control the Ship. You've uprooted us from our own world and brought us to this one, but we have some say in our safety. And yours, too. I'm afraid I can't let any of us go down there alone until we've worked out all the possibilities.'

I really thought he was going to hit me for a moment, his anger was so great. Anyway, he controlled himself and turned away from me and looked down at the city once more. Susan looked at me anxiously. She had a healthy respect for her relative and obviously hated it when there were any arguments. The Doctor turned back and astonished me with a genial smile.

'We'll go back to the *Tardis* and have some food and discuss it then.'

I nodded and jumped off the boulder, handing down Susan and Barbara. I looked up at the Doctor who was taking one last look at the distant city. The rays of the sun just caught his eyes but I had a sudden impression that something else was making them shine. I tried to dismiss the feeling that came to me but it clung stubbornly. I was in a new and unreliable world and it didn't help to think that the least trustworthy factor was the Doctor.

The light was fading when we got back to the *Tardis* and I became anxious because Susan had dropped behind. All of us were as sure as we could be in the circumstances that there was nothing to fear in that dead place, but I didn't much care for the way darkness was closing in. I imagined Susan blundering about for hours, perhaps even all night, trying to find her way back. The Doctor and Barbara went back into the Ship and I started to look for her.

My feet made no sound as I tramped through the wood, the only occasional noise being when I happened to touch a twig or one of the branches and it snapped and powdered around me. It was eerie and uncomfortable because I had the distinct feeling that someone was watching me. Twice I stopped and turned round quickly, feeling a slight prickling of the hairs on the back of my neck, only to curse myself for an over-sensitive imagination.

Suddenly I heard a cry of sheer terror up ahead of me and the sound of wildly running steps. It was a part of the forest we'd passed through before and we'd left plenty of shattered wood behind us. I heard the running feet snapping and breaking the dead wood underfoot and then Susan ran into view. I caught her in my arms and she sobbed gratefully.

'A hand touched me,' she gasped. 'I was picking one of those flowers I found, the crystallized ones and the hand just came out from behind me and touched my shoulder.'

'But you know nothing could be in this forest, Susan.'

I helped her along the path leading back to the *Tardis* and it was several seconds before she answered me.

'*We're* in the forest. Why shouldn't someone else be?'

I told her it must have been a branch that she'd backed into but she wouldn't have a bit of it and neither the Doctor nor Barbara could make her change her mind.

'It was a hand, a human hand. I didn't imagine it and I didn't make it up. I tell you there are other people in the forest besides ourselves.'

We were gathered around what the Doctor called the food machine and the Doctor finally rapped on the top of it, stopping both Barbara and myself in the middle of further arguments with Susan to try and make her see she was wrong.

'It doesn't matter now anyway, because we're not going to stay on this planet. Whether Susan felt anything or not is a little mystery we'll leave unexplained.' He looked at me. 'Chesterton, as soon as we've eaten I shall operate the controls and we'll go somewhere else. Perhaps back to your own planet Earth. How would you like that, eh?'

After the silence Barbara said quietly, 'Can you do that, Doctor?'

He shrugged. 'As I told you, the computer that calculates the journeys is out of order. Its behaviour is too erratic for me to make any promises. And remember, we have not only space to cover but time as well.'

I saw a pulse quickening on the side of Barbara's throat. 'Do you mean you may never take us back to our time on Earth?' she demanded. The Doctor nodded.

'I mean exactly that, Miss Wright. But don't let us pursue that line of conversation any longer. I'm sure you're both hungry; I know I am. What would you like to eat?' He looked at me inquiringly.

'Anything? Anything in the world?' I asked.

'Yes, even on your world."

'I think I'd like some bacon and eggs, then, if that's all right with you?'

He waved a hand, as if he were the head waiter at some exclusive restaurant and I'd asked him whether he had such a thing as a fork. He stood in front of the food machine and pressed a variety of buttons.

'XL4 285 J,' he muttered. There was a moment's pause and then a little bank of bulbs lit up and we heard a buzzer sound three times. The Doctor lifted a flap and produced what looked to me like a Mars Bar on a paper plate, except that it had the colour of white icing. He handed it to Barbara, turned back to the machine and intoned the same numbers and pressed the buttons again and then handed me a similar plateful. Barbara and I glanced at each other doubtfully and Susan laughed.

'Go on, try it. It's all right,' she said, her eyes sparkling with amusement. I bit into mine, not knowing quite what to expect and there I was eating eggs and bacon! I could taste the two things quite distinctly and the food was just preserved at the right heat. I felt the Doctor waiting for me to say something.

'The eggs are a bit hard,' I said casually and winked at Barbara. The Doctor wasn't even put out.

'You should have told me. I'd have adjusted one of the

numbers by a fraction. It's all very easy. Susan, what will you have?'

Susan shook her head. 'I'm not hungry, Grandfather.'

He looked at her sharply. 'That's unlike you, my child. Still, I won't press you. For myself…' He turned his attention to the machine again and it was as if he were surveying a tray of hors-d'oeuvres… 'I shall have some of that Venusian Night Fish we discovered. I'm very glad I laid in a supply of that.'

He muttered some numbers and letters and extracted a paper plate with three long rods on it, a little like bread sticks. I asked him how the machine worked and how I was able to taste the eggs separately from the bacon.

'Perfectly simple, Chesterton. Tastes are very much like colours, you know. You blend two to get a third and so on.'

It was at that moment that we all heard the tapping. I was just about to take my last bite and my hand froze near my mouth. It was a distinct noise, one-two-three on the doors of the Ship. The Doctor put down his food on the machine and hurried away.

Susan said: 'I told you there was someone in the forest.'

We went after the Doctor and found him in the control room operating the scanner. The pictures on it changed and changed again as he searched around outside, but whatever had been responsible for the noise had totally disappeared.

'I have very strong searchlights accompanying this picture,' he told me. 'They're quite invisible outside the *Tardis*, of course. They merely serve to make a picture possible at night-time. Well, there's nothing there now, at any rate.'

He switched off the scanner and smiled at me in the most guileless fashion. 'It would seem to support what I said about leaving this planet.'

He made me feel uneasy but I agreed. There was something behind his face and I couldn't for the life of me think what

43

it was. He motioned to Susan to stand nearer to him and his hands began to run over the dials and switches as I had seen him do before. This time, however, the engines, or whatever power-force it was that drove the *Tardis*, didn't respond in the same way. All I could hear was a complaining growl blending in with a screech as if gears were being changed badly. Susan looked at her grandfather anxiously and he shook his head.

'Have a look at the fault locater, Susan.' Susan ran away and Barbara moved nearer to the Doctor.

'Doctor, it isn't broken, is it?'

He looked at her benevolently. 'No, Miss Wright, not a bit of it. We'll soon track down the fault.'

Susan had been peering into a small glass panel and even from where I was standing I could see numbers spinning round inside it.

'K Four, Grandfather.'

'One of the fluid links.' The Doctor moved around the control column slightly, beckoning me to join him. He lifted up a panel and I bent down beside him. I could see a small row of glass rods nestling together side by side. He lifted out one of them and asked me to hold it while he fixed his glasses more securely on his nose. Then he took it from me and tapped it.

'Yes, this is the one all right. This is similar in a way to a fuse that you would employ to conduct and control your electricity on Earth.'

'What's the matter with it?'

'Mercury is the conductor in this case, not little pieces of wire.' He held it up and showed me one end of it. 'The end has become slightly dislodged and the mercury has escaped.'

'So all you need is to replenish it with more mercury.'

He beamed at me as if I'd propounded the theory of relativity to him. 'I couldn't have put it more succinctly myself, Chesterton.'

'Can I get it for you?'

'I'm afraid you can't, no.'

I stared at him in bewilderment. 'Why not?'

'Because I haven't got any.'

There was a fairly long silence as he and I stared at each other. I looked right into his eyes and now I knew exactly what lay in them, but there wasn't a single thing I could do about it. Barbara broke the silence.

'But surely you carry a spare supply of mercury, Doctor?' He shook his head sadly.

'There's none left. I used the last of it for some experiments about a month ago. A trifle foolish of me not to replace the stock, but there it is.'

'Haven't you got a barometer that you could…?'

'Nothing like that at all, my dear young lady,' he interrupted. He examined the fluid link as if searching for an answer then shrugged his shoulders in despair. It was all most convincing if you had an unsuspicious nature. I stood there, waiting patiently for the Doctor to work his trick. His playacting obviously fooled Barbara because she touched his arm gently.

'Don't worry about it. It isn't such a tragedy.'

'Ah, but that's just it, I *am* worrying.' He moved about slowly, gesturing with one hand in a most dramatic way. 'Miss Wright, Susan, Chesterton…' he surveyed us all with sombre eyes, '… because of my absent-mindedness in not renewing my stocks, we are destined to live out the remainder of our lives on this inhospitable planet.'

I glanced across at Susan and her eyes seemed to fill her face. I thought it was a bit cruel of the old man to play on his own granddaughter's feelings, too.

Barbara said, suddenly, 'What about the city? There may be some mercury down there.'

The Doctor stopped in his tracks and swung his head round

at her. His mouth dropped open and then he crossed to her and wrung one of her hands with joy.

'My dear, of course! The city! This business of the fluid link had quite put it out of my mind.' He darted a look at me and the triumph in his eyes was as clear as daylight. 'Even you can't object to that, Chesterton.'

I was conscious that they were all looking at me.

'No, we'll go down to the city. Doctor,' I replied as calmly as I could. 'There isn't any other choice, is there?'

'I'm glad you take that attitude, though it's too dark to go now.'

I nodded in agreement. I just had to accept the situation he'd contrived. For all I knew he had pounds of mercury all over the *Tardis* but there were too many places he could hide it and far too many other things he could interfere with and use as excuses to make a journey down to the city.

I fancy the Doctor could read the way my mind was working, searching for a way out and not finding one, because he came up to me and tapped my chest with his fore finger.

'Only one Captain of the ship, eh?' Then he turned away briskly and added, 'At first light then.'

I decided to profit from this early evidence of the Doctor's ability to get his own way and mark it down for future reference. Barbara and I followed Susan on a tour of the Ship. There were two lavish bedrooms and four smaller ones and two beautiful bathrooms. I spent half an hour in one of the bathrooms playing with a machine that shaved you and trimmed your hair. It was a bit weird at first, feeling a small machine the size of a half-crown and about as thick as a marshmallow buzzing away independently all over my chin. Later the Doctor showed me how to attach the shaver to another piece of equipment, a metal skull-cap with two metal supports on either side of it which clamped themselves on the shoulders. The skull-cap then fitted entirely over the head but was raised about four inches above the hair. The Doctor then 'took a reading' as he called it of my hair style and length and made some adjustments to the programme of the little round shaver and attached it to the inside of the skull-cap. It was distinctly uncomfortable to have that little machine gliding gently over my hair but I got used to it and five minutes later when I took the contraption off my shoulders I had as good a barbering as I would have received at Simpson's in Piccadilly.

The Doctor then showed me how to operate the oil and water shower, a machine that was an eight-sided pillar which enclosed me and directed a thousand jets of water and what the Doctor called muscle oil at me. I felt as if I were being pummelled furiously by tiny fists. The Doctor's explanation of this invention was that the sharp jets of hot water opened up the pores of the skin and allowed the oil to penetrate the surface; then they were washed out by a second jet of water and the process continued. Eventually, nerves and muscles begin to respond to the 'pummelling' treatment and flex and relax as each jet hits the skin, getting more concentrated exercise than in one full day's movement and being toned up and massaged at the same time.

I slept exceedingly well that first night in the *Tardis* and when I woke up in the small bedroom that had been assigned to me, I found that my clothes were neatly spread out on a low table. My suit had been cleaned and pressed and the other clothes newly laundered. I found my companions up and dressed and drinking glasses of what looked like tomato juice and tasted of melon. Susan told me it was a concentrate of what she called the winter berries of Mars. The Doctor was very business-like, packing up a few items for our journey, mostly little boxes of food and two cartons of what he described as concentrated water.

I'd done some pretty serious thinking before I dropped off to sleep after the oil and water shower the night before. Secretly, I knew that I was beginning to enjoy what was happening to me. It was a fantastic wrench, to be literally heaved out of one's normal way of life and have nothing much in the way of compensation but doubt and uncertainty, yet already a part of me welcomed it. I'd enjoyed teaching but I knew it wasn't right. The job I'd failed to get at Donneby's was only one instance of a line of similar tries and failures to find the answer, not just to my future but to my own personality. That was all over and now I could work out the restless itch that had made me scratch my way through a dozen jobs. I could fill myself with excitement and adventure with the Doctor and then, when the day came for it to end and he returned me back again to Earth (and I was quite sure that he would, one day!), I'd be happy to settle down to some ordinary work with no regrets.

But Barbara? I had no way of knowing if she felt the same way and no reason to suppose that she did either. Suppose the wrench was too great for her to accept? She had a strong personality, I didn't doubt that for a minute, and had certainly shown she wasn't lacking in courage. I looked at her as she finished off her breakfast drink, composed but pale, very silent and withdrawn, and wondered exactly what effect the happenings were having on her. I crossed over to her.

'All right?'

'Yes, but I didn't sleep too well I'm afraid.'

'Not quite the bed you're used to?'

She smiled briefly.

'I'm not heading for a fit of hysterics or a nervous breakdown.' She knew what was in my mind, all right.

'A sort of headache,' she went on. She finished off the drink. 'Susan had a touch of it too, so it couldn't have been the unexpected food. Or the change of scene,' she ended dryly.

I saw Susan turn the door switch and the now familiar lights blazed out strongly and died down again as the great doors began to swing open. The Doctor beckoned us to follow him and I took Barbara's arm.

'If you don't feel up to it, say so. I'll bring you back.'

'Oh, I'll be all right. Besides, Susan and I have had some medicine the Doctor gave us. I really feel better now.'

I saw Susan and the Doctor step out of the Ship and Barbara and I followed slowly.

'Do you know,' I said, 'that we don't even know what the Doctor's name is?'

'He doesn't respond to personal questions very well.'

'Maybe not, but I have two I'm determined to ask him when I get him in the right mood – What does he do and who is he?'

There was a short silence. I said, 'Perhaps that's what we ought to call him – "Doctor Who?".'

'All I want to know is where he and Susan come from,' said Barbara.

Susan suddenly appeared at the doors.

'There's something out here!'

CHAPTER FOUR

The Power of the Daleks

We went out after her quickly and found the Doctor staring down at a bright metal object that glittered in the morning sunlight. It certainly hadn't been there the night before.

'What do you make of this, Chesterton?'

It was a small metal box affair about the size and shape of a library book. I picked up the firmest looking stick I could find and although I could feel it crumbling in my hand it lasted long enough for me to tap and poke at the box.

'You're wise to take precautions,' said the Doctor. 'It does look rather like a booby trap, doesn't it?'

I decided to risk it and picked up the box. The lid came off easily enough, although I was still very apprehensive and slid it off as slowly as I could. The Doctor took the box from me and we all stared at the contents. It was full of little glass phials.

'They look like capsules of medicine,' said Barbara. The Doctor nodded his head, replaced the lid and handed the box to Susan.

'I agree. Put them in the Ship, Susan, and I'll examine them after we get back from the city.'

Susan ran into the Ship and the Doctor heaved his little haversack containing the food rations around his shoulders a little more firmly.

'Whoever did that tapping we heard last night dropped that box,' he murmured. 'It suggests some sort of civilization. An advanced society, able to work metal, make glass and construct things out of those materials. The evidence doesn't suggest hostility,' and he noted my nod of agreement with his theorizing. 'But, nevertheless, we'll keep a sharp eye open.'

Then Susan came out and locked the doors of the Ship and we started out for the city.

It took us about an hour to get through the forest, climb over the ridge of boulders and cross the sandy desert to the outskirts, and in all that time none of us saw a bird or an insect or any living thing at all. The city made up for the labours of the journey, for we were all thoroughly tired out from ploughing through the ashy sand that sometimes reached well over our ankles and made walking a slow and cumbersome business. Always we had those magnificent buildings in our eyes and they grew larger and larger until at last we reached the first one. I call them buildings for want of a better description but really the whole design was as if someone had commissioned Frank

51

Lloyd Wright to build a city and then someone else had come along and pushed thousands and thousands of tons of ashy soil all around it, leaving only the roofs and other protuberances, and then laid a metal floor over the soil and pressed downwards. The first proper rest we had was when we were able to step out of the ash and start walking on the metal flooring.

The constructions, for I started to call them this rather than buildings, pierced their way out of the metal and had neither doors nor windows. I estimated that the total area of the city must have covered two square miles at least and not one of the constructions seemed to be duplicated. There were some that were merely rods sticking upwards for about thirty feet, others that were square boxlike affairs and several round ones as big as gasometers, all made of the same dull metal and showing no joins or screw holes whatsoever.

The Doctor seemed to know where he was going and forged ahead of us, darting his head from side to side and muttering an occasional 'Ah!' or an 'Oh!' as if each fresh sight explained its most secret use to him. At one time he stopped and motioned us all to silence. We stopped chattering about what such a place could be for and who could live in it.

'Something moved on top of one of those round buildings over there,' he said sharply. 'I saw it out of the corner of my eye.'

We stood there watching for several minutes, but nothing happened and eventually the Doctor led us forward again, driving deeper into the heart of the city.

Suddenly, as we all walked round one of the squarer shapes, we saw a flat building with a short ramp leading to what was undoubtedly a doorway. The Doctor rubbed his hands with glee and actually gave a little dance.

'It has a pattern, this place, Chesterton,' he chortled. 'I guessed it from the first and I was right. That building with the door is the heart of the place and now we'll see the inside and discover what's going on.'

'It's mercury we're after, remember, Doctor.'

'Yes, yes, yes,' he replied irritably, 'but now we are here we might as well explore a little.'

Barbara put her arm out and leaned on me for a moment and I became aware that there was perspiration on her brow and her face was not looking as healthy as it might. I helped her over to the doorway and sat her down in the shade of the building and turned to the Doctor grimly.

'You can see she isn't up to this, Doctor. Let's find the mercury and get her back to the Ship.'

'I'm all right,' said Barbara stubbornly, but Susan and I glanced at the Doctor. To give him his due, he was immediately and genuinely concerned.

'Then you rest here my dear,' he said gently, 'and we'll take a little look inside.' Barbara shook her head and got up.

'We'll find it better if we split up,' she said. 'I'm perfectly all right I promise you. Let's each look for some instrument or other and meet back here in fifteen minutes.'

I didn't want to agree but I knew Barbara would go on arguing until she got her own way. There was a resolution about her, a determination that didn't want to admit any weakness and none of us wanted to make an invalid out of her by wasting time. The Doctor agreed to her plan on behalf of the rest of us eventually and we went through the door.

We found ourselves in a fair-sized hall or chamber which had several doors on it. Actually they were less doorways and more like arches with a steel plate closing them off. At the side of each lintel was a small flat bulb and it was Susan who discovered that if you passed your hand over the bulb the steel plate slid away and revealed the corridor beyond. We each chose a door and checked our watches. I noticed with a mental smile that the Doctor had a typical gold hunter on a thick chain. He could have walked into any Edwardian drawing-room and not been out of place.

The door I chose didn't seem to lead anywhere at all; it was just a short corridor with one corner that ended in a blank metal wall. I retraced my steps back to the entrance chamber again and found Susan, who had the same sort of story to tell. Almost at the same moment the Doctor appeared and told us he'd had some success, so we followed him and he showed us a little room he'd discovered that was filled with recording instruments rather similar to the oscillation meters used to map sound frequencies. There were thirty of them, ten to each wall and the needles of each one differed slightly in its journey as it wavered over the slim strip of metal that revolved underneath it.

We went from one to another, examining each in silence and puzzling over them. There weren't any numbers or letters anywhere in evidence and without a clue to the reason for the machines I began to examine them for any signs of the mercury the Doctor needed.

Suddenly I heard a gasp behind me and whirling round I saw the Doctor stagger into the centre of the room. Susan ran to him and clutched his arm.

'What is it, Grandfather? What's wrong?'

'I can read the messages on these machines,' he said, hoarsely, and on his face was a look of absolute horror. 'You must forgive me, Chesterton; all of you must! What have I done with my stupid subterfuge?'

'What are you talking about?' I demanded, suddenly anxious at his genuine concern.

'We must go back to the Ship immediately. No wonder that young woman didn't feel well.' He glanced down at Susan and I saw tears in his eyes. 'Neither did you, my child.'

He stared across the room at me, his eyes distended and his

hands working away at his collar as if it were strangling him.

'Don't you understand, Chesterton,' he gasped. 'Air pollution! That's the purpose of these machines. Somehow or other they are capable of testing a sample of air for thirty miles around the city.'

For the first time, I noticed a sheen of sweat on the Doctor's forehead. I remembered how Barbara had looked.

Susan said, 'But we've been able to breathe all right, Grandfather. What's the matter with the air?'

'I don't know that. I only know that the oxygen content of the air is being shared with some other substance. Miss Wright has been feeling unwell. So have you.' He looked at me searchingly but I shook my head.

He leaned against one of the machines wearily.

'I have felt something. An unaccustomed tiredness. No, no, Susan,' he went on as his granddaughter put a hand on his arm anxiously, 'it's the other one I'm worried about. We must find her and get back to the *Tardis*. Go out and look for her.'

Susan slipped out of the room. The Doctor waited until the door slid into place behind her and then raised his eyes to mine.

'You knew I deliberately interfered with the fluid link, Chesterton, didn't you? So that I could get my own way and explore this city?'

My silence served as a sufficient answer. I was too worried about the rapid way he was weakening. He levered himself away from the machine slowly and accepted the support of my hand.

'Get us back to the Ship, Chesterton. And thank you for not… giving me away to Susan.'

He began to have difficulties with his words and started shaking his head from side to side as if trying to keep awake. It was rather like watching a slow motion film of a boxer who had just left himself open to a straight right to the point of the jaw. I put an arm around him, waved my hand over the bulb and negotiated him through the doorway.

'Susan!' I shouted, but there was no sign of her and I half walked, half carried him up the metal corridor and out into the entrance chamber. I still couldn't see Susan anywhere and thought the best thing to do would be to get outside that building and, if necessary, leave the Doctor and collect the others together.

Suddenly I saw something moving out of the corner of my eye and at the same moment Susan came slowly backwards through the front entrance. I became aware of a low humming in the air, very similar to the noise that telephone wires make in the country at night. Susan stopped and looked round her wildly and then stared at me, her eyes distended in a dreadful sort of horror. She looked past me and I knew that there *was* something behind me somewhere. I was just about to turn and look when the Doctor collapsed in my arms. I laid him down on the floor in a sitting position and looked at Susan, a question forming on my lips.

The answer came through the front entrance slowly. A nightmare answer that had the blood draining away from my face and the skin stretching around my eyes. It was a round metal thing about five feet in height, like an upturned beaker with a domed top. It had dull metal flanges all round it and three different kinds of rods sticking out in front. It glided over the metal flooring and Susan retreated before it until she stood close to me. Now I knew what it was I'd been conscious of, and what Susan had seen behind me, because I became aware that we were surrounded by more of them, all gliding out of the doors of the entrance chamber and pointing their rods at us.

Except from one door, one door that was tantalizingly open and unguarded. All I could think of was that the Doctor was seriously ill and needed help.

One of the machines came quite near to us and then stopped about four feet away. I started to examine the three rods it had, battling to control the fast way I was breathing and every impulse I had to panic and run. The three rods were each entirely different. The first, and shortest, was attached to the top, the domed part, and seemed to be a sort of eye. I could see the iris contracting and expanding as it ranged over us. The other two were in the position of arms, being roughly in the centre of the 'body', at each side of it. The left-hand one was a stubby barrel affair, little more than a stick with a hole running through it. The other, the longest of the three, was a black rod with a suction pad at the end of it. I also noticed that there were two bulbs on either side of the base of the 'eye-stick', and at first I thought that these were two more eyes until they suddenly started to light up as the machine spoke.

It spoke! I was so startled that I took a short step backwards and nearly fell over the Doctor's body. The voice was all on one level, without any expression at all, a dull monotone that still managed to convey a terrible sense of evil.

'What are you doing here?'

Susan seemed to have conquered her fear of the machines and it was just as well because I couldn't have found the ability to speak if I'd been offered a fortune.

'My grandfather is very ill,' she said. I detected the slight uneven quality in her voice but I had to admit it was very slight. Her control was admirable and she seemed to improve as the amazing conversation went on.

'Why?'

Susan looked at me in a bewildered fashion and then shrugged helplessly.

'What does it matter why? Isn't the fact that he is ill enough? Help us.'

The thought of these malignant things bringing out stretchers and drugs didn't seem likely to me at all but I bided my time. The doorway was still unguarded.

'Why is he ill?' grated the machine, as if it had taken no notice of what she'd said. I decided it was time I took a hand.

'It's the air. We've just discovered it makes us ill when we breathe it.'

The eye-stick turned and regarded me. There was a pause of about five seconds, then the machine began to move backwards slightly and then stopped.

'You will all rest in a compartment we shall show you.'

'But my grandfather is ill! Desperately ill for all we know. Can't you help us?'

The machine ignored her with a chilling repetition of its earlier statement and I thought I heard a more ominous note in the words. Nothing that one could describe as an expression exactly but more a sensation of definite command rather than the plain statement it had been.

I bent down and started to lift up the Doctor, motioning Susan to help me. As she bent down, my lips were close to her face.

'One of us must get free,' I whispered. 'Can you see that doorway? Can you get away?'

'You do it,' she breathed. We made quite a play of making the Doctor seem heavier than he really was. 'Take his key. In his top right waistcoat pocket. Bring back tablets from the drawer in my room in the *Tardis*. Bottle marked "stimulizers".'

We gradually got the Doctor to his feet and he wasn't completely unconscious because I could see his eyelids fluttering and his lips moved spasmodically, although no sound came. Susan tucked one of her hands under his left arm and took the weight and I pretended to be holding him up as I slipped my fingers into his waistcoat and took the key she'd told me about.

I winked at her and then let go of the Doctor and ran for the unguarded doorway. Immediately the machines spun round towards me and I heard a loud crackling sound. Something hit my legs just behind the knees and I crumpled to the floor in a frenzy of pain, suddenly and horribly aware that my legs were completely paralysed. I heard a short scream of helpless agony and realized that it was me who was making the noise. Pain stabbed up inside my legs, right up through my body. There was a terrible, burning sensation at the base of my spine and then again at the back of my neck and I blacked out.

The first person I saw when I woke up was Barbara. In turn I saw the Doctor and Susan. Barbara and the Doctor were both asleep or unconscious (I squashed the idea that they might be dead immediately), but Susan was very wide awake. I could see the marks of dried tears on her cheeks and her hair was disordered. I looked around me quickly and took in the room. Apart from one low shelf upon which the Doctor lay the room was devoid of any sort of furnishing at all. It was a square box of a room, made entirely of metal. I could see one archway and guessed rightly that it was the entrance. I couldn't see any sign of one of the door bulbs that opened it and realized we were prisoners. I tried to get to my feet but my legs simply gave way. Susan came over to me quickly and gently pushed me back to the floor.

'Don't try to use your legs. Please don't try.'

'But they're dead! No life in them at all.' I stared at her in absolute panic. 'I can't do anything. Don't tell me I'll never use my legs ever again…'

She stopped my almost hysterical outburst with a finger over my lips.

'Hush! You'll use them again,' she murmured. 'The Daleks told me that the effect was only temporary.'

My heart stopped pounding quite so much and I felt the fear beginning to ebb away. Susan gave me a sad little smile but I found it comforting.

'At least they haven't killed us,' she said.

I suppose I ought to have accepted that as some consolation, but I didn't, simply because I couldn't believe that wasn't their ultimate intention. Daleks, Susan had called them. I asked her to explain.

'I don't know much more than that. We're right under the city and we were brought down here in a lift. Barbara was in here when they pushed us in.'

'How is she?'

'Not as bad as my grandfather,' she replied seriously, 'but she's ill. You and I seem to have escaped.'

'Except for my legs.'

'One of those sticks they carry is a gun of some sort. It projects a charge of electricity, I think. That's what they hit you with. I spoke to one of the Daleks when we came down in the lift and it told me that they have built this city and that they think we're called Thals.'

'Who are they?'

'I don't know, Mr Chesterton. I'm just telling you what I heard. I gather that there are two races on this planet – or used to be at any rate. The Dalek race and the race of Thals. The Daleks thought all the Thals were dead until recently and then their instruments began to record movements in the forest.'

'Could that have been us moving about?'

'No, this was quite a while ago. I'm afraid they think we're enemies who are determined to destroy them. I tried to explain that we aren't these Thals and that we aren't enemies at all but then the lift stopped and I didn't have time to talk any more. They've given us some food and water and it tastes perfectly all right. In a funny sort of way, I think they're afraid of us.'

I digested this and it began to make sense. If there were only one race on a planet, or at least they imagined they were the only race, and then they learned that there were others, I suppose they might react as the Daleks had done. The thought kept repeating itself in my brain that what had happened to my legs was only temporary and I looked round the room, searching for some inspiration. Above the door, I suddenly noticed a small metal box with six glass balls set in it that glowed slightly. I had no idea what it was for but I marked it down for future examination.

The door slid open and one of the Dalek machines slid into the room, stopping just inside the doorway.

'If you are not Thals,' it grated out, 'you will not have any drugs.'

'We aren't Thals,' I replied.

'But if you are, you must be immune to the polluted air. We are immune because of the casing we wear.'

The thought that there was someone or something inside the machine hadn't occurred to me and I found it intensely interesting. I'd simply thought of them as machines.

'You live inside your machines all the time?' I ventured.

'The Thals must have a drug to ward off the polluted atmosphere,' the Dalek persisted. I suddenly felt Susan's hand grip my arm.

'Drugs! The metal box we found outside the Ship.' She turned towards me and I could see the excitement in her eyes.

'Don't you see? That tapping we heard must have been one of the Thals. It dropped a box of drugs and that's what we found.'

'And the drugs have the power to ward off whatever it is that's in the air, Susan. It may be able to cure the Doctor and Barbara.'

The Dalek had been listening to all this patiently enough but now broke in on our conversation.

'We are interested in these drugs. We may be able to rid ourselves of these protective suits and leave the confines of the city and rebuild the planet. You know where some of the drugs are to be found?'

'We found some,' I replied cautiously. We wanted the drugs for ourselves, not for the Daleks.

'One of you will bring the drugs to the city.'

The Dalek began to glide backwards. I shouted out to it that we needed help to get back to the forest but the door slid shut. I forgot about what had happened to me and tried to get up and promptly fell down again.

I stared around me miserably. The Doctor and Barbara totally out of action, and although the air hadn't affected me I was practically useless. That left a fifteen-year-old girl as a

62

balance between life and death, which gave us about as much chance as a 500 to 1 outsider has of winning the Derby. Susan had plenty of courage and intelligence but she was scarcely suited to what lay ahead. I looked across the room at her, bathing the Doctor's head with water from a metal pitcher and thought how small and defenceless she seemed.

The door slid open and the Dalek came into the cell again. At least I thought it was the same one. None of them had any distinguishing marks so it was impossible to tell.

'One of you will fetch the drugs. It has been decided.'

'We're all ill,' I said savagely. 'Can't you see you're asking the impossible?'

'The girl is the fittest,' the Dalek droned back in its inhuman way. Susan looked at it and I saw how startled she was. I suppose it had never occurred to her that she would be chosen to go. The Dalek began to speak again.

'The girl will start immediately. We have considered the question of the four of you. You may not be of the Thal race. There seems to be no reason for you to lie about it. Yet you resemble them in many ways.'

Susan said, 'How do you know? I thought you said that you believed the Thals were all dead. How do you know what they look like?'

'We know how they will look,' was the enigmatic answer. 'They will be much worse than you.'

I tried to work out exactly what the implications were. Worse than us? Yet we were like them in many ways. The Dalek began to speak again.

'The chemical in the air can affect the structure and shape of human tissue. The race of Thals must be mutations. If they are in the forest where you say you have the drugs, you must be on your guard against them.'

Susan stared at me in horror and all I could do was look

back at her helplessly.

The Dalek glided forward a few feet towards Susan.

'You will start immediately.' Again I heard that slight emphasis, the warning note behind the words.

After the silence, Susan said, 'Must I go?'

I couldn't bear to go on looking at her, I felt so helpless. Instead I glared at the Dalek.

'She's only a child!'

'She will start immediately!' This time there was no mistaking the menace in the words. Susan came across to me and I held her in my arms.

'You'll have to go, Susan. You can see how it is. The others need the drug desperately and my legs are useless. Just go straight there and straight back.' I kissed her gently on the forehead. Then I held her head close to mine so that I could whisper to her.

'Hide some of the drugs. The Daleks will take them all when you get back if you don't.' She nodded slightly against my chin and then got to her feet and faced the machine.

'I'm ready.'

The Dalek moved backwards and Susan followed without even a glance back at me. The door descended and she was gone. I heard the Doctor muttering again, rambling on about the fluid link, a series of disconnected words and phrases that only told me how much his conscience must have been troubling him, even in his illness. Barbara didn't make any move at all but just lay there on the floor, for all the world as if she were in a deep sleep.

For all the world! That phrase which I could use so thoughtlessly on Earth now came home to me. I wasn't on any world I knew, any that I could trust. I was in alien surroundings, a prisoner and forced to give a man's job to a girl of fifteen.

I pounded at my useless legs with my fists in a fury of rage and resentment, but it didn't do me any good at all. Hope seemed a far away thing and life a gleaming comet in the sky that was rapidly burning itself out.

CHAPTER FIVE

Escape into Danger

About two hours later the pain started to twist my stomach in knots and I knew that the poisoned air was beginning to work on me. It didn't make any difference that both my legs were a mass of pins and needles which told me the feeling was returning to them. My clothes were sodden with perspiration and after a while the room started to do cartwheels. I remember crawling over to Barbara when she started moving her head from side to side and making little sounds of pain, because I had some idea of bathing her face with water. I never made it, of course, and the worst of it was I knew I'd even failed to do a simple thing like that. Then the floor did some more leap-frogs over the ceiling and I lost consciousness.

The first thought I had when my eyes opened was that passing out was something that was happening a little too frequently to be funny any more. The stomach pains had gone, and my head was clearing rapidly, although I had the very devil of a pain in my left arm. My watch was clearly in view and I was shocked to see that over five hours had gone by since Susan had left. At that moment a cool hand was laid on my forehead and Susan was staring down at me.

'I want you to rest for a few minutes,' she said quietly. 'I've brought back the drugs and given you all some so everything's all right. All you have to do is relax and you'll be fine again.'

'What kept you?' I managed to ask.

It seemed to me as I were speaking perfectly naturally but Susan told me later that I croaked so much I sounded as if I'd been in a desert without water for two or three days. Probably I was too relieved that things had turned out for the better to notice.

Susan's story was an extraordinary one and she told it to us, as we lay there together gathering our strength, without any false heroics or affectations at all and my admiration for the girl increased a hundred-fold.

'The Daleks piloted me to the edge of the city,' she began, 'and then one of them gave me a little push with its sucker-like rod and I nearly fell on the ashy sand stuff. They told me they could only travel over metal and actually I was rather glad because I was a bit frightened they were going to go with me all the way and find out about the Ship. I couldn't see them clambering over rocks and things but still I was a bit nervous until they told me I was to go on alone.

'I ran across the desert part as fast as I could and climbed through the rocks. Just as I was beginning to think the worst was over, the storm began. It was really frightening, great flashes of lightning and huge raindrops. And I lost my way.'

She looked at me with those huge eyes of hers and I began to get quite carried away with her story. I could see her running through that forest of dead trees, being absolutely drenched by the rain and then discovering that she hadn't an inkling where she was or which way to go to reach the Ship.

'All I could think about was what Mr Chesterton had said to me just before I left. "Straight there and straight back," he'd said.' She smiled at me very slightly. 'I could hear those words above the storm and the wind and they stopped me huddling down somewhere and gave me a kind of courage. And my stars! I needed all the courage I had, Grandfather, because even in all the noise and concentrating on trying to find some landmark, I began to realize I was being followed!'

She couldn't complain about our lack of interest. The Doctor was bending forward slightly from his sitting position on the bench and Barbara was sitting up with her arms clasping her knees, while I couldn't take my eyes off Susan as she walked about telling her story and punctuating it with small, precise little gestures.

'I remembered what the Daleks had said about the Thals being mutated and I had visions of some four-headed, six-armed monster lumbering after me. Well, I was determined I wasn't going to be a nice little luncheon for anybody and I raced along, not knowing much about where I was going but hoping against hope I'd be lucky. As a matter of fact, I wasn't far out at all, although I'd circled around the Ship a little. Anyway, I broke through the trees at last and there was the Ship in that sort of clearing place. I rushed over to the door and unlocked it and banged it shut behind me. Grandfather, I was saturated and I'm afraid I've left pools of rainwater all over the floor.'

The Doctor smiled at her slightly and moved a hand to forgive any imagined misdemeanour.

'I think that was the really dreadful part,' continued Susan, 'knowing I had the drugs, or what we hoped were the drugs anyway, and at the same time being aware that there were… things outside the Ship.'

'Did you turn the scanner on?' demanded the Doctor and Susan nodded.

'Of course, and I could see something moving in the trees. It had a scaly look about it.' She clasped her hands in front of her and then brought them up to her face slowly.

'Well, I knew I had to go out there. The only sort of weapon I could find to defend myself with was one of your walking-sticks, so I took it and tucked the drug box in the waistband of my trousers and went out of the doors again.

'The rain and the wind had stopped by this time, but it had become very dark. Now and again there was a flash of lightning. I didn't quite close the doors behind me in case I had to retreat quickly, and I stood there looking around. Just to the left of the Ship there's a flat rock behind some trees and I caught a movement in one of the lightning flashes. I was just trying to work out whether I could make a dash for it when I heard the voice.

"'I will not harm you," it said. "Do not be afraid of me."

'I asked him who he was and he said, "I am Alydon, of the Thal race. Have you taken the drug I left for you?"'

'Left for you?' echoed the Doctor. We all looked at each other, working out the implications. Susan clapped her hands together and sat down at her grandfather's feet.

'Yes, Grandfather, Alydon had left the box of drugs for us. He hadn't dropped it by accident as we'd imagined. Anyway, this all sounded promising so I asked the voice if it would come out where I could see it.

"'You may show yourselves to your three companions," Alydon replied, "but that is because you accept each other, just as my race and I accept each other. Yet I and my people are mutations."

"'You sound all right," I said.

"'Have you taken the drug?" he insisted, so I explained what had happened, all about the Daleks and everything. There was quite a long silence and then a terrific glow of lightning that lasted for every bit of ten seconds and I heard the one who called himself Alydon give an exclamation.

"'You seem to be like us. This is the first time I have seen you clearly."

"'Then step out where I can see *you*. I have to get back to the others. They are held prisoner and I'm not sure whether I can trust you or not yet."'

Susan looked over at Barbara and I saw quite a mischievous glint in her eyes.

'There was a bit of a pause and then Alydon stepped out of the shadows. The daylight was coming back a bit now and although the lightning was moving away it still flickered on and off sufficiently for me to see fairly clearly. Well, I don't know what they mean by mutations on this planet, Barbara, but he's the most wonderful looking man I've ever seen anywhere in any world.'

The look on my face must have been a bit extraordinary because both Susan and Barbara laughed at me.

'Present company excluded, of course,' giggled Susan. I bowed, feeling ridiculous, and if you've ever tried to bow when you're sitting on your haunches you'll know exactly what I mean.

'Be objective, Susan!' urged the Doctor.

'Alydon is about six foot four and perfectly proportioned and he has long fair hair. The scaly thing I'd caught a glimpse of is the cloak he wears.' She glanced at Barbara again. 'I'll come back to Alydon later, if you like,' and Barbara raised her eyebrows to agree to a future and secret conversation.

'Anyway, Alydon walked with me through the forest and gave me another box of drugs just in case the Daleks wanted a whole box to themselves. He asked me a lot of questions about the machines and the city, most of which I couldn't answer, but we agreed that I'd talk to the Daleks about the Thals and arrange a sort of truce.'

Susan leant a hand on her grandfather's knee and looked up at him. 'You see, the Thals have come searching for food, so I promised I'd arrange with the Daleks for them to give him some.'

'So you made an arrangement with the Daleks, did you?' the Doctor said very quietly.

'Oh, yes,' said Susan happily. 'I told them all about the Thals and what they wanted and the Daleks said they'd let them have a supply of food and water. Those machines aren't half as bad as they look, you know.'

The Doctor patted Susan's head gently and got to his feet. His eyes met mine briefly and there was a thoughtfulness about them that made me uneasy.

'Go on, Susan.'

'Did I do something wrong?'

'I don't know, my child. Just tell me everything that happened.'

'The Daleks dictated a letter for me to write to the Thals,' she faltered. 'They gave me a sheet of thin metal paper and a sort of stylus. It just said that they'd leave a stock of food and water in that entrance hall where we were captured and the Thals could come and collect it.'

The Doctor sunk his chin on one hand, supporting his elbow with the other. His expression wasn't unkindly but it was undeniably serious.

'And how,' he said quietly, 'were the Thals to know it wasn't a trap?'

'I told them I'd sign my name to it.'

'Which you did?'

Susan nodded miserably. The old man moved several paces away and I could almost hear his brain ticking over.

'And when are the Thals to collect the food?'

'Tomorrow morning, when the sun rises.' Susan got up and ran to him and threw her arms around him.

'Oh, Grandfather, what have I done? Something awful, I know I have!'

He stroked her hair gently.

'Susan, I'm afraid you may have placed these Thal people in jeopardy. I don't trust the Daleks and we have no reason to. On the other hand, I do trust the Thals. This Alydon of yours seems to have kept his wits about him. Leaving drugs for us. Keeping watch. Giving you an extra supply. These are two entirely different races. The one tries to imprison us, and when we are incarcerated do they make any effort to relieve our suffering? Not at all. They find out we have access to drugs and they send you for them. But they do so because they want the drugs for themselves!'

The Doctor looked at us all gravely.

'Why should these Daleks share what they have with anyone else? Can any one of you show me even a small hint that they possess compassion or mercy or friendship? Are they even *interested*? I can't believe it.'

Just above the Doctor's head, I could see that little box with the six glass eyes set in it. What else could it be, I argued to myself, but a television camera or some sort of microphone? Probably both. If the Daleks were overhearing everything we were saying, the best thing we could do would be to shut up and not make our feelings so clear. I was so busy working all this out that I didn't realize the Doctor had been talking to me directly.

'I said, "What's the matter with you, Chesterton?" I don't believe you've heard a word.'

I got up from the floor and circled around him so that my back was to the box. Then I was able to gesture with my hand under cover of my body. I pointed back urgently with my thumb.

'If the Daleks could see or hear you, Doctor,' I said, pretending to be angry, 'how do you think they'd react? They haven't killed us and they let us use the drugs, and you can't blame them for being suspicious. Give them time, Doctor, they'll soon prove how friendly they can be.'

The Doctor wasn't slow-witted. He simply nodded his head after his eyes had slid past me and taken in the box. Then he bent down and picked up the metal water pitcher and held it out threateningly with one hand while the other, hidden by my body, gestured me to retreat.

'Are you daring to argue with me, Chesterton?' he blazed and I started to move backwards. The two girls, who hadn't any idea at all what we were up to, started to remonstrate with him and I saw Susan moving with the idea of taking the weapon away from him and that was the last thing we wanted. I back-pedalled a bit faster and the Doctor came after me, his eyes gleaming with hatred as he waved the pitcher dangerously.

'After all I've done for you, to have to stand here and listen to you defending our enemies.'

I meant to fall anyway but I did it a little sooner than I expected because something tangled up my legs and I had to twist to save myself. I was able to see the Doctor raise the pitcher and throw it with unerring accuracy at the box on the wall. It hit it dead centre and there was a short flash and a puff of smoke and the box hung shattered.

The Doctor bent over me, beaming with pleasure and helped me to my feet.

'Excellent, my boy, excellent. The perfect team, eh?' He turned and explained to the others while I picked up the thing that had tripped me up. It was a long cloak with the pattern of scales all over it and made up of some material I'd never come across before. It seemed to be like a cross between silk and rubber yet it was of the texture of cigarette paper.

Susan said, 'That was Alydon's cloak. He gave it to me because it started to drizzle again just as we reached the rocky ridge.'

'Come along, both of you,' interrupted the Doctor. 'Before

one of those machines comes in to find out what happened to their apparatus. We've got to get out of this prison.'

'And warn the Thals,' said Barbara quietly. The Doctor glanced at her but didn't answer her.

'What do we know about the Daleks?' I asked.

We all thought for a moment.

'Those eye-sticks of theirs seem to have a wide range of vision,' murmured Susan, 'and they carry a powerful kind of gun.'

'As I know only too well,' I said, 'but how do they work? The suggestion is that the Dalek himself lives inside the machine, or the protective casing as they call it, yet there must be some sort of motor. If we could find out the principle of the engine, maybe we could attack it in that way.'

The Doctor rubbed his nose thoughtfully. 'Yes, you've hit the centre of the problem, Chesterton. This whole city, you know, is made from metal. There are even metal floors. Also, they told Susan they could only travel as far as the edge of the city.'

'And they work on electricity,' put in Susan.

'But how, my dear? Here we are walking about on the floor and not getting any shocks or anything. How are they drawing up their power?'

Barbara said, 'Then there's that slight, electric smell they have about them. You know, it reminds me of something and I just can't put a name to it.'

She thought for a moment then looked up, her eyes gradually opening wider.

'Dodgem cars! You know, Ian, in the fairgrounds. That smell is exactly the same!'

'I wonder if…' began the Doctor, then he moved over to me and took Alydon's cloak out of my hands and ran the tips of his fingers over it. He looked up at me.

'Do you think the Daleks have discovered how to operate by using static electricity, Chesterton?'

Reason made me want to argue, but then I thought of movement through time and space and the change of dimensions inside the Doctor's Ship. You can't really argue when you have those things at the back of your mind. I shrugged. The Doctor grinned at me and patted my arm.

'That's right, my boy, always keep an open mind. I know the use of static electricity may seem absurd but it is an answer, isn't it? Well, if they do, they only have one point of connection. They draw the current from the floor and pass it back again. Now, supposing, Chesterton…' He spread the cloak out on the floor and Barbara interrupted.

'Supposing we pulled the Dalek on top of the cloak?'

'Exactly, Miss Wright.'

'Will the cloak insulate, Doctor?'

He and Barbara examined it together and I reminded them that Susan said that Alydon had given it to her because it had started to rain again. And there was no doubt that it had a rubbery sort of feel to it. Susan sat down on the floor and took her shoes off and started to pick off some of the ash from one of the heels.

'Well, we must try it,' decided the Doctor. 'Chesterton and I will do all the work. You and Susan keep well out of range.'

'Actually, what I was thinking, Doctor,' I said, 'was that either Susan or Barbara could jam something in the door. We have no guarantee that the Dalek is going to enter the room, but if we make the door stick he might be curious enough to come in.'

'Good idea, but you do it. Sit here and as soon as the door opens stick something right at the base of the pivot. The door slides sideways, doesn't it, up and then into the right-hand wall?'

I nodded.

'Doctor, I don't know whether it's occurred to you yet,' said Barbara, 'but the Dalek's eye-stick can practically see all around it. You haven't much chance of creeping up on it.'

She held up her hand and showed a lump of what looked like streaky plasticine.

'Unless you use mud.'

The Doctor came back to me and helped me pick up some of the fragments from the floor that had fallen out of the broken wall box.

'We can't go far wrong with this sort of co-operative enterprise,' he murmured to me and then suddenly I saw the door start to open.

Immediately we darted about all over the place. I crouched down as near the door as I could and the Doctor flattened himself opposite me, Susan and Barbara stood in front of the door, directly in the path of the Dalek.

As soon as the door was fully opened, I pushed the little piece of soft metal I'd bent off the box into the corner of the door. The Dalek stayed out in the corridor, apparently suspicious of us.

'You have destroyed our communication system,' it rasped. 'You will all stand together.'

Nobody moved. The Dalek advanced until it was half-way through the door. It still wasn't near enough the cloak for my liking.

'Why are two of you on either side of the entrance. All four of you must be together!'

The Dalek obviously decided it was time to illustrate what would happen if nobody took any notice of it. I saw the short, stubby rod point towards one of the empty corners. There was a harsh crackling sound and a jet of blue sparks shot across the room blistering the wall and twisting and melting it until little rivulets of molten metal ran down and pooled on the floor. The Doctor and I glanced at each other and moved over to join the girls reluctantly.

'It has not been decided,' the Dalek stated, 'whether the communication system was broken deliberately or by accident. It does not matter. You are no longer of any interest to us. We have tested the drug.'

There was a pause as we all looked at each other in bewilderment. The voice of the Dalek suddenly broke in, evidently realizing further explanation was necessary.

'Several of the Daleks upon whom the drug was tried failed to respond to it and have died. The drug, then, is poison to us. To be able to rid ourselves of these protective suits and go out and rebuild the planet Skaro, the Daleks must increase that chemical in the air which is alien to you and to the Thals.'

'But if you do that,' spluttered the Doctor, 'you'll kill everybody else.'

'The planet belongs to the Daleks.'

I stared at the machine in horror.

'But you're all right in the city. You've got the suits. Surely there's enough room for you and the Thals?'

'For a short time, perhaps. But as we multiply and as the Thals multiply, the conflict between us will grow. We will demand more of the chemical air and the Thals less of it. So they must be exterminated.'

There was another pause as the eye-stick surveyed us each in turn.

'The decision as to your future,' it said at last, 'will be made tomorrow. After we have shown the race of Thals our power.'

The Dalek moved backwards smoothly and the door started to close. Then, as the door descended on to the piece of metal it stopped abruptly. The Dalek waved its sucker-stick over the eye on the outer wall but the door still refused to budge.

It advanced into the room. I noticed that the gun-stick was directed at Barbara.

'Remove the block on the door.'

I didn't have any choice in the matter and I went over and threw the little piece of metal away. The Dalek glided out. Our plan had failed. Then Susan had an inspiration and shouted, 'Bring us some more water. It's all gone and you can't leave us all night without it.'

'It will be brought later.'

The door slid down.

Susan's brainwave meant that the Dalek would return, but we had to wait three hours before he did, though the machine that brought our water may well have been a different one. Anyway, the door slid open and it trundled into the cell without any suspicions at all. We were all sitting about on the floor, the Doctor half asleep and Susan and Barbara playing some word game that I was amazed to find had Susan an easy winner. Apparently lexicography was one of her strong points.

As soon as the door opened I saw my chance because I was nearest to the door and rather to one side of it. I pretended to be asleep and as the machine sailed in I leapt up and pushed it from behind as hard as I could. It rolled over the cloak and stopped and Barbara jumped out of range of the gun-rod and smeared the mud she'd kept tacky right over the lens of the eye. I could hear the voice of the Dalek squawking but this time the words were quite indistinguishable, as if someone was being choked. The Doctor had woken up immediately and we all got out of the way of the front of the machine, well out of danger in case the gun-stick was still operating.

'Susan,' ordered the Doctor, 'find another bit of metal and jam that door open. Miss Wright, go with her and keep watch along the corridor. Chesterton, you and I are going to see if we can get this thing open.'

Barbara and Susan moved off and he and I started to examine the outer casing, looking for some sign of a hinge or a join. We found it eventually in the front, about a foot from the top and directly in the centre. There was no movement or noise from the machine at all, so we put our hands to one of the metal flanges and lifted up the top.

I don't like to think about what we saw inside. It was an evil, monstrous shape. There was one eye in the centre of a head without ears and with a nose so flattened and shapeless it was merely a bump on the face. The mouth was a short slit above the chin, more of a flap really, and on either side of the temples there were two more bumps with little slits in them and I heard the Doctor mutter that they must be the hearing parts. The skin was dark green and covered with a particularly repellent slime. I felt my stomach heaving and I bit the inside of my mouth until I tasted blood. The Doctor viewed the thing with repugnance and wiped a hand over his brow.

'This is awful, Chesterton, but we must get it out of the machine.'

After the silence, I said: 'Because I've got to get inside?'

He looked at me keenly. 'Yes, my dear boy. It's the one hope we have. Can you do it?'

I was saved from answering because Susan wanted to come back and have a look at what we'd found. She took some persuading to stay with Barbara but at last the Doctor succeeded. Barbara's eyes met mine and she knew that what we'd found was a secret she wouldn't want me to share.

The Doctor came back from his argument with Susan, which had culminated in a direct order, something Susan always obeyed; and together we pushed the machine off the cloak. The Dalek started to move! I saw its head begin to raise slowly and was suddenly aware that it had two short stubby arms about two feet long and that one of them was moving towards a lever.

Then the Doctor pushed the cloak inside the machine and we lifted the thing out and bundled it into a corner. It was the most dreadful and horrifying experience I've ever had and I could see it had affected the Doctor, too, because he constantly licked his lips as if his mouth had gone dry, and his cheeks had a rather grey look about them.

'Chesterton, if I had any doubt at all about what we were contemplating, the sight of that disgusting thing has totally dispelled them. And they call the Thals mutations! Now then. How do you feel about riding in the machine, eh?'

Naturally, it was a tight squeeze. The Dalek machine was about five feet in height, but by crouching down and pressing my arms to my sides, I could just make it. There were several levers and switches inside but I had no idea which worked the individual rods.

'I'm a bit afraid to try these out, Doctor,' I said, 'in case they have some communications system or other.' The Doctor was busy wiping mud off the eye-stick.

'Well, you won't need them. We'll replace the lid on top of you and push you along and make it look as if we were simply following you.'

He called the other two back and together they lowered the lid over my head. I could breathe well enough and I found that by turning my head slightly I could get one eye near enough to a rubber eye-piece and have a wonderfully clear view ahead and around me, very much like normal vision.

'Try speaking,' I heard Barbara say.

'Yes, all right.'

'We can hear you well enough,' murmured the Doctor.

'But make it sound more like a Dalek,' said Susan.

I tried to imitate their flat, expressionless voices and Susan's face appeared in front of me, smiling and waving a hand in triumph.

'That's marvellous, Mr Chesterton.'

I felt a movement as they pushed me and we started to move towards the door. The Doctor went ahead and used the sucker-stick to guide the way and we turned into the corridor and moved down it.

It was a tremendous relief to leave that room, but as the others turned the machine round to move it out, I caught a glimpse of the bundle under the cloak. I could just see a small green hand with three fingers struggling weakly to lift up the material that covered the body. The fact that it failed and fell limply to the steel floor didn't make me feel any better.

At that moment, they pushed me round a corner of the corridor and my blood went cold. About twenty yards ahead of me I saw a Dalek machine and it began to turn and face us.

CHAPTER SIX

The Will to Survive

The Dalek in front of me stopped moving and I tried not to think about what would happen if it fired. The Doctor was ahead of me and a little to one side, pretending to be urged forward by the long rod with the sucker attachment. But he would be right in the line of fire. I felt I knew how men in the Tank Corps suffered when an enemy bazooka suddenly appeared.

'Steady, Chesterton,' I heard the Doctor whisper, and then he raised his voice angrily. 'Stop pushing me, confound you! I'm going. I'm going!'

We came to rest about six feet away from the Dalek and I was quite certain I wasn't going to do any speaking first. I was too afraid of making a mistake. I kept thinking about the way the wall had melted in the cell. A bead of sweat ran down my forehead, trickled past my left eyebrow and ran down my nose.

'They are going to level eight?'

I detected a slight lift at the end of the sentence as the Dalek spoke and it was the first time I had noticed real tonal quality in their speech.

'Yes.'

The Dalek examined us all for a few seconds then began to swing away.

'There have been no instructions. The matter will be referred.'

I thought desperately and didn't come up with anything.

Then the slight figure of Susan appeared in my eye-line.

'I won't go!' she shouted. 'You've no right to keep us prisoners!'

She started to run, making to go past the other Dalek and along the corridor. The machine startled me with its speed of movement. It whirled round and I saw the sucker-rod extend outwards and bury itself in the wall just ahead of Susan, stopping her abruptly.

'Go back to the others.'

Susan turned slowly and stood next to her grandfather and Barbara appeared on the other side of him. The Dalek turned its eye-stick towards me and I saw its bulbs flashing.

'I will help you move them into the lift room.'

I didn't dare say anything. Those flashing bulbs reminded me that I hadn't any idea whether mine were working or not. The Dalek extracted its suction pad from the wall, swung round and passed the pad over one of the bulbs on the wall. A door slid open and Susan stepped through it. Barbara stood directly in front of the Doctor so that he could grip one of the rods on my machine and pull me. We must have been inches away from the door. Barbara had already gone through when the Dalek's eye-stick suddenly shot downwards and looked where I imagined the Doctor's hand was holding my machine.

'Step away! Take your hand away!' The Doctor lifted his hand and, of course, I came to rest. The eye-stick turned to me.

'What is wrong? Are you damaged?'

I decided stubbornness was the best approach.

'They are to go to level eight,' I intoned. There was an indecisive pause and then the eye-stick wavered and the body of the machine swung away. The Doctor seized his chance and pulled at one of the rods on my machine, and eased me through the doorway, then he pushed me around so that I faced outwards. The Dalek turned slowly, the eye-stick's lens enlarging and contracting.

The Doctor waved his hand on the inside wall-bulb and the door began to descend. I watched it as it moved downwards, expecting every moment for it to stop and then start opening again when the Dalek reached the conclusion that it was being tricked, but all that happened was that I heard its voice briefly announcing into what I could only imagine was some sort of internal microphone system that the prisoners had been sent up to level eight. Then the door closed and the sound of its voice was cut off.

The Doctor bent down on his knees, examining the wall-bulb.

'Give me your shoe, Miss Wright,' he said.

Barbara took one off and handed it to him and he smashed the bulb to pieces with the heel. Then his hand darted inside one of his waistcoat pockets and pulled out, of all extraordinary things, a button-hook, and I saw him insert it into the hole he'd made in the wall. He probed about for a few seconds and drew out a couple of wires and, giving them a sharp downward pull, broke them. He sat back on his heels, replaced the button-hook in his pocket and rubbed his hands together.

'I don't think they'll open this door again in a hurry.'

'Perhaps you could get me out of this tin can then.' He got to his feet, beckoning to the two girls urgently. 'My dear fellow, you must be roasting in there. The hinge is at the front, Miss Wright.'

They gradually eased the lid open and I scrambled out thankfully. We were in a small sort of ante-room, little more than a large cupboard, really, and facing the door we'd just come through was an open lift.

'Well, I'm glad to get out of that thing,' I murmured. 'Now I know how sardines feel.'

'Come along, come along, we must get up in that lift and get away from the city,' said the Doctor sharply. Suddenly we all heard the distant sound of alarm bells, and then Susan tugged at my sleeve and pointed to the door. Part of it was beginning to glow red and a small hole was forming. The Daleks were burning their way through!

With one accord we scrambled into the lift and Barbara selected the top one of the twenty buttons laid out in a panel on the inside. The lift began to shoot upwards. Susan looked at her watch.

'It's nearly six, Grandfather. The Thals will be arriving at any moment.'

The Doctor made a non-committal noise in his throat and avoided looking at any of us. Barbara gazed at him steadily and I thought she was about to say something when the lift began to slow down. Then it stopped altogether.

We moved out and found ourselves at the top of a building, one of the round, gasometer-type ones, I thought, and directly facing us was a wall of glass that domed over our heads, giving an impression of the top floor having been designed as an observation place. It certainly gave us a marvellous view of the city and I guessed we were every bit as high up as the top of the Eiffel Tower. We walked over and surveyed the scene.

From above, the city lay spread out like a fantastic collection of engineering inventions. We were clearly in the highest building of all and as we moved along the corridor I began to get a better picture of the sort of country surrounding us. In the distance I could see the forest where the *Tardis* lay. It looked strangely comforting. On a line with it, starting at the ridge of rocks where Susan had first seen the city, there was a gradual descent and then the ground began to flatten out. I could see the beginnings of dense vegetation. Moving away still farther on another side of the city there was a line of enormous mountains that towered over us.

As we moved around the observation floor we came across what I can only describe as an example of Dalek sculpture. It was little more than a series of metal squares welded together, without any particular design or pattern, and since it had no attachments to the flooring or showed that it possessed any internal engines or served any purpose at all, we concluded it must be some form of bizarre decoration.

The Doctor moved us all back to the lift again and held a council of war.

'Now we've seen several of these lifts. The only thing we can do is go down in one and try and break through the city.'

Barbara said, 'Do you think we'll be able to avoid the Daleks?'

'I'm sure of it, Miss Wright. Remember that Susan has told us the Thals are coming to the city. The Daleks will be occupied with them. With care, we ought to be able to slip through to the forest.'

'I thought so!' said Barbara, angrily. 'I knew that's what was in your mind. Never mind about the Thals coming here because we've arranged it or that we know they've tried to help us. All you can think of is to use them as red herrings while we run for cover!'

The Doctor looked surprised at her outburst and I must say it startled me. Ever since I'd met her I don't believe she'd lost her poise or her self control, even when she came face to face with the metal beast in the forest and thought it was still alive. The Doctor recovered himself.

'Miss Wright, I'm not interested in your comments. We have our own safety to consider.'

'You really mean to say you'd sacrifice these other people without giving it a second thought?'

'Well, of course I've thought about it,' he replied sharply, 'but our duty is to get back to the Ship.'

'Our duty to whom?'

'To each other,' the Doctor said.

The trouble was that I agreed with both of them. I knew what the Doctor was driving at and we were hardly cut out to defend the Thals in any battle that the Doctor obviously anticipated was going to ensue. At the same time it did go against the grain a bit to walk away without at least warning them. I was just about to put all of this into words when the lift behind us started to disappear out of sight.

'Quick!' shouted the Doctor. 'No time to argue. They'll be up in that lift in a moment.'

I ran over to one of the statues and manhandled it to the lift entrance.

'What are you wasting time for, Chesterton?'

'I'm not wasting time,' I replied curtly. I was a bit fed up with him for always thinking the worst of people. 'I'm cutting down the odds a little.'

Barbara helped me with the statue and we pushed it over the edge. It slipped out of sight and cautiously I craned my head into the aperture and watched it hurtling down the lift shaft. There was a terrific crash beneath and I saw a cloud of smoke billow out. I stepped back and winked at Barbara. The Doctor patted me on the shoulder.

'I'm sorry, my boy. I judged you too harshly.'

'There's another lift over here Grandfather,' called Susan, about twenty feet away. We moved over to her.

Barbara stopped suddenly and then ran over to the glass.

'They're coming! Look – there's a whole party of them!'

Round the corner of one of the square buildings came a magnificent old man, wearing one of the cloaks that Susan had brought back from the forest. He was easily six foot four or five and wore a kind of coronet on his head made of some very bright silvery metal. He was clean-shaven and very bronzed and his hair was pure white and short-cropped. He was obviously the leader; I could tell that by the signals he gave to the party of men behind him, cautioning them to be watchful and not to go too quickly.

We hammered on the glass to try to attract their attention and then we all tried shouting together, but the observation chamber was obviously soundproof, and anyway we were much too high up for them to notice us.

Barbara said, 'We must help them, Ian.'

There was a short pause while the Doctor looked at us each in turn. Eventually, I took my eyes off the little group of men and nodded slowly.

'All right. We'll all go down in the lift. The Doctor will take you and Susan back to the forest. I'll warn them. We can meet up later.'

'I want to go with you,' she protested.

'You do as you're told,' I said roughly. I didn't like being rude to her but it was the only way I could think of shortening the conversation. Barbara tightened her lips and moved away to the lift we had chosen and I followed with the Doctor, who was shaking his head from side to side.

'Sentimentality, Chesterton. That's all it is. Still, I won't stop you.'

'After all, Grandfather,' said Susan hesitantly, 'it was my fault that the Thals came here in the first place.'

We stepped into the lift and travelled the rest of the way in silence. When the lift stopped we crept out cautiously. I took the lead, the two girls in the middle and the Doctor bringing up the rear, and we moved in this Indian file fashion through another little ante-chamber and into the corridor, closing the door behind us.

The particular corridor we found ourselves in was obviously

a main one and was nothing more than a series of cross-roads, with other corridors cutting across it, so it was a constant question which way to take. I decided to keep in a straight line and it was very fortunate that I did so because after about only two or three minutes we came into a small entrance hall and saw an open door, leading out into the city. I edged my way forward, telling them all quietly to stay where they were at the end of the corridor until I'd found out how safe it was. The outside of the building was totally deserted so I beckoned to them.

'All right, Doctor. You can just see a part of the ashy ground over there. I've lost my bearings, I'm afraid, but I think the forest is away to the left so you may only have to circle a bit. There's only one other thing I want to say.' I looked at Barbara. 'The Doctor's quite right in one thing. There can only be one leader. Do everything he tells you. I'm only breaking away now because… well, perhaps because we owe the Thals something. Otherwise I'd take the Doctor's orders and no arguments.'

Barbara's eyes flashed dangerously.

'If that's intended for me, it was a waste of time,' she said coldly. The Doctor found my hand and shook it.

'Do your best, my boy, but make all haste to the Ship, won't you?' I nodded and smiled at Susan. Barbara walked away without another word. I watched the Doctor peer out of the doorway, take Susan's hand and then the two of them disappeared. Barbara paused and then looked back. We stared at each other for a second or two, then she followed the others.

I leant against the wall for a moment, wishing I had a cigarette. It was the first time I'd really been alone since Barbara had appeared out of the fog on the Common. I couldn't hide the fact that there was a slightly cold feeling at the back of my neck and it would have been comforting to have someone with me to work out what to do next.

90

I didn't have a cigarette and I was on my own, so I had to get on with it. The Thals had to be warned of possible danger and told to get out and get out quickly. I looked around me. No hope here. The best plan was to move outside the building.

The opposite direction to the one the others had taken led me deep into the city, and just as I was beginning to think I was lost I caught a glimpse of the first building we'd all found when Barbara had shown her first real signs of illness. I dodged from building to building carefully and stopped every few paces to search all around and above me, but there wasn't a sign of a Dalek anywhere. I eased my way along a smooth metal wall to the entrance of the building and peered in.

The entrance hall where we'd originally decided to split up was considerably changed. All sorts of boxes and cartons were piled up in the centre of the chamber and there were also a number of metal carboys filled with what I guessed was water. The Thals were grouped around them and the leader was peering into one of the boxes and picking out some packets and examining them. Finally, he replaced them and indicated to one of his men to help him climb up on to one of the smaller crates.

I noticed that all the men looked strong. They were all taller than average and broad in proportion, and they all had very fair hair. All of them wore the same kind of cloaks and tightly-fitting trousers of some light brown colour which seemed to have the texture of leather. From the knees downwards I could see that a pattern of holes had been cut in the trousers about the size of shillings. On their feet the Thals wore a simple sandal with one thong through the first and second toes and then encircling the ankle and joining the sole at the back of the heel. Apart from the difference in features, there was no way to tell them apart and only the leader wore anything different at all – the silvery coronet on his head.

The leader looked around him.

'Daleks!' he called. 'We come to you in peace. We have no way of repaying you for this food except by working with you. Together we can level the ground outside your city and make things grow in the fields. Rain is falling more frequently and there is every hope that the planet Skaro can be rebuilt. We shall take the food now and leave you our grateful thanks. Later we shall return and find out how we may work together.'

Suddenly I saw just the tip of a Dalek sucker pad edging its way out of one of the doorways. I flashed a look around the chamber and saw more Daleks. I could smell the evil in the air; it was like a poisonous gas that set every nerve on edge and sharpened every instinct. I jumped forward into the doorway.

'It's a trap!' I shouted and all the Thals wheeled round and stared at me. 'Don't just stand there…'

A Dalek shot out of its hiding-place about thirty yards away and I saw its gun-stick swivel and point at me. I threw myself sideways and rolled away desperately, hearing the short, sharp crackling sound as the gun's ray flashed across the chamber. The wall behind where I had been standing a split second before blew up in smoke and fumes, melted and blistered.

There was immediate pandemonium. The Thals began to panic, turning and bumping into each other, and the Daleks emerged from the shadows. The Thals' leader was the only one who had any presence of mind at all. He raised his arms above his head and his voice rolled around the chamber and brought everything to a standstill. 'Stop! I command you!'

Amazingly, everything did stop. The Thals stared up at him and the Daleks, all of whom were in view now, came to rest in a rough semicircle around them. The leader looked round the room and there wasn't a trace of fear on his face.

'There has been enough war on Skaro,' he said quietly. 'Our two races are the only survivors. What is the point of further destruction?'

He folded his arms and gave every impression of confidence and authority. Here he was, unprotected and unarmed, defenceless in a ring of dangerous enemies and yet there was no suggestion of pleading in his voice, no hint of fear or cowardice. More than that, he was making his authority felt. It breathed around the chamber like a blast of cold air, demanding common sense and reason to pay him attention. It was absolutely magnificent and for sheer, naked courage I have never seen anything like it.

'We can work separately, going our own ways, developing different cultures, amassing new thoughts and ideas, customs and habits until such time as they collide and argue with each other. Or we can work together, learn from each other, share the hardships and the discoveries. I tell you, *this is the only way!*'

There was a silence and the leader waited for his answer. When it came it brought a shiver of horror down my spine and I felt all my nerves and muscles bunching together. I heard one Dalek voice grating out from somewhere.

'The planet Skaro is ours. And ours alone.'

I saw thirty gun-sticks raise themselves slightly and point at the leader. As if realizing his danger he made one last attempt to exert his personality.

'Daleks! We come in peace!'

The moment he had finished speaking thirty blue streaks of flame sped out from the machines and hit him simultaneously. For one single second his body was illuminated with a pale glow so that he shimmered as the lines of a ship do on the horizon. Then he crumpled and fell into the boxes and cartons beneath him.

'Run!' I screamed. The Thals started to race past me out into the city. I turned and fell and a Thal's hand lifted me up.

'Don't wait,' I said savagely. The Daleks were beginning

to sweep after us, fortunately delayed by the crates they had scattered about.

The Thal still held on to me until I was safely on my feet again. We ran out of the building together. Ahead of us I saw one of the Thals suddenly crumple up and crash to the metal roadway. A small group of Daleks appeared out of another building and the Thals scattered, taking one of the turnings to the left. The Thal I was with pulled me into a safe place behind an upright metal pole about six feet thick.

'Haven't you any guns?' I asked him. 'Didn't you bring any protection with you at all?' He just looked at me, rather pityingly, I thought. Then he searched the buildings behind us.

'This way seems to be clear.'

'Back to the forest?'

He nodded.

'We'll be out of range there, I think.'

I saw one of the Thals being chased along a little alley between two short, square buildings by a pair of Daleks. They caught up with him and pinned him to one of the walls with their suckers. I could see his face quite plainly, his mouth opening and closing and his eyes wide apart with fear. They fired into him and I turned my head away in disgust. The Thal beside me pulled at my arm.

'We must go. It is senseless to stay here watching.'

'It was senseless to come here at all without taking any precautions,' I shouted at him. He frowned and shook his head at me, as if I were talking gibberish. Over his shoulder I watched a Dalek machine swing round slowly, obviously attracted by the sound of my voice. I decided it was time to get as far away as I could.

We managed to get out of the city without any further incident and joined up with what was left of the main group, who were resting in the desert strip between the city and the forest. I suppose there were about twenty of them and they looked in the last stages of exhaustion. None of them spoke much and they all seemed dispirited and downcast, although they were considerably relieved when the Thal I was with joined them.

'This is the man who tried to warn us,' he told them. 'My name is Alydon,' he went on, as we sat down with the others.

'Oh, you're the one who met Susan in the forest and gave her the drugs.'

He nodded and turned to introduce me to another Thal who sat down beside me.

'This is Ganatus.'

He nodded to me briefly and then looked at Alydon.

'Alydon, you are the leader now that Temmosus is dead.' Alydon looked back at the city without saying anything.

'We lost about seven men, including Temmosus,' Ganatus went on.

'The others must be warned. We must move from this area,' murmured Alydon and started to get to his feet. I stopped him.

'Look, before you go, have a talk with my friend the Doctor. We've already immobilized one of the Daleks. They aren't invincible, you know. We can work out some sort of plan to defeat them.'

The two Thals exchanged glances and I could see how puzzled they were.

'Alydon, you can't just let your leader die for nothing,' I argued.

'No, I agree.'

'Well then. Let's all work together. I'm sure we can find a way to beat the Daleks.'

'You mean that we should fight them?' he replied, and the astonishment in his voice was crystal clear.

'What else?'

'That is impossible.'

'But I thought you needed food?'

'Yes we do, and that's why we asked your companion Susan to intercede for us.'

'Yes, I'm sorry about that because it was through her you were trapped…'

'We would have gone to the city in any event,' he interrupted. 'But we can't fight the Daleks.'

'We won't fight them,' put in Ganatus.

I stared at them in amazement.

'But why not?'

'What you are suggesting is that we engage in a war with them. War is alien to us. So is fighting of any sort.'

'That's all very well but—'

Again he interrupted me. 'Under any circumstances.'

'But Alydon,' I persisted, 'the Daleks aren't human beings. They're just evil, half creatures, half machines, determined to destroy you. Do you really imagine they're going to leave it like this? They'll find a way to come out of their city and destroy you in time. You know they will.'

Alydon nodded. 'Yes, we must move to another area.'

'No! They'll follow you wherever you go. They're determined that no one else shall inhabit this planet except themselves. Alydon, they've told us this. The very air you breathe is death to them.'

There was a silence for a moment or two. I thought I was making some impression on them so I ploughed on.

'I'm not saying you should destroy them completely, but you've got to show them you're at least as powerful as they are.'

'Which means fighting them,' said Alydon.

'Yes, probably. You know what the alternative is. They'll exterminate you, every one of you, without giving it a single thought.'

There was another, longer pause.

Alydon said, 'If what you say is true there is only one thing left to say.'

I waited. Ganatus stopped looking at Alydon and stared down at the ashy soil, running a little of it through his fingers. Alydon stood up and his eyes met mine.

'The Daleks,' he said quietly and with a terrible sincerity, 'will have to exterminate us.'

CHAPTER SEVEN

The Lake of Mutations

The Thals had made their encampment quite near to the *Tardis* and, at first, when we arrived there were cheers and laughing faces from the women and children and the older men. I went over and joined the Doctor, Susan and Barbara and we all listened as Alydon related the events that had taken place. The Thals grouped themselves in a semicircle round Alydon with the children in the front rank and the mothers and single girls kneeling behind them, while the remainder of the men stood at the back. I noticed that nobody asked questions; they just seemed content to wait for the story to be unfolded.

At Alydon's feet sat the other Thal I had met, Ganatus, and a young woman whose name was Dyoni. Susan told me she was to be married to Alydon. Like the men, all the female Thals were perfectly proportioned and their hair was fair. As I watched the girls listening to Alydon's story, I reflected that they were very much like a cluster of different jewels. Each one with her own sparkling beauty yet each one different. Of them all, Dyoni was undoubtedly the rarest gem. She wore her hair several inches longer than the other women, well below her waist and gleaming like fine spun gold in the sunlight that speckled through the dead white trees. The average height of the female Thal was about five foot six, but Dyoni was just under six foot and she had a superb dignity and grace which offset her height. I noticed she wore a small coronet on her head which bore some resemblance to the one the Thal leader, Temmosus, had worn. Susan whispered that she was his daughter.

I didn't know what to make of them. Alydon's words echoed and re-echoed round my brain yet I couldn't seriously believe that any person would willingly accept death rather than make some struggle. I whispered as much to the Doctor and he led us away until we were out of earshot. We sat down in a little glade and Susan produced wax cups of water and some food she had laid ready from the Ship.

'From what I gather,' said the Doctor, as he tackled some of his favourite Venusian Night Fish, 'the Thals are the survivors of a terrible war. I have been talking to some of the elders and I think I can piece the threads of their history together. Two hundred years ago there was a vast atomic explosion here that destroyed all living matter but left buildings and construction intact. Because of mountain ranges and other things of that nature, some parts of the planet escaped the worst effects and the people who happened to be in those areas lived. It must have been a miserable existence for them because they had little food in stock and the air was poisoned as well.' He finished his food and dabbed at his lips with his handkerchief. I offered some more food to Barbara but she looked away coldly. I imagined she still hadn't forgiven me for speaking so abruptly to her in the city. The Doctor broke in on my train of thought.

'The result was mutation, Chesterton, as you may well have guessed, and that must have been the most terrible hardship of all. To discover that the offspring were ugly and deformed, to ask each other why it had happened and to know that there was only one possible reason – war.'

I had never seen the Doctor more serious.

'War between whom?' I asked.

'Why, the Thals and the Daleks, my dear boy, without any doubt. The Daleks built that city out there and others like them and then exploded their bomb. The trouble was, the bomb was a million times more powerful than they'd imagined. It seems that this is the only city with any living thing in it that the Thals have found as they've wandered over the planet, so that'll give you some idea.'

Barbara said, 'Then why have these Daleks survived?'

'The mountain range, Miss Wright. It deflected the greater part of the radiation. It was the same with those survivors of the Thal race, too. They have come from a valley thousands of miles from here, a valley totally surrounded by enormous hills, I understand.'

'But surely the Daleks weren't always the way they are now, Doctor?' I said.

'No, Chesterton. You see, the Thals battled on with a drug they managed to evolve, which warded off the poisoned air.

They perfected it until it was able to cure them from any disease at all. As time went by, with each successive generation, they gradually came round in full circle. What we see now is the result of total mutation. They weren't unattractive people in the beginning, you know, but now they have eradicated ugliness and awkwardness from their bodies altogether.' He paused significantly. 'And from their minds as well.'

'But the Daleks haven't,' said Susan.

'Precisely, my child. The Daleks encased themselves in those protective suits. They became acclimatized to the poisoned air without realizing it. Now they need the poison just as we and the Thals need good, fresh air. So the mutation cycle has not completed itself and the Daleks are as you and I have seen them, Chesterton.'

I made an expression of disgust.

'Are they as bad as that?' asked Susan.

'Like something out of a nightmare.'

'Well thank goodness we shan't meet them again,' she said. Barbara got to her feet and walked away slightly. The Doctor watched her carefully, then his eyes met mine. I raised my eyebrows but he shrugged eloquently. I knew him as an expert in summing up a situation and producing a solution with uncanny accuracy, but I also knew that he was not likely to hazard a guess about Barbara's feelings. Or any woman's for that matter. I got up and strolled over to her.

'You're pretty quiet, Barbara.'

She started to break pieces of a branch off a tree and crumble them between her fingers, but she made no attempt to answer me or even give any indication that she knew I was anywhere within a mile of her.

'Look, I know I upset you in the city. Will you accept it if I say I'm sorry I spoke harshly to you?' I touched her arm lightly.

She twisted away sharply and faced me. I could see a tiny pulse hammering away in her throat and her whole body seemed to be trembling with suppressed anger.

'Don't you dare touch me!' she half whispered at me and there was such venom in the way she expressed the words I was completely startled. I have never been brilliant at hiding my feelings, unless I have it well worked out in advance, and obviously my face betrayed how surprised I was.

'I suppose you imagine I like having you hanging around me all the time. Well you're wrong! We're forced together, I can see that, but that doesn't mean to say I have to like it!'

'But, for heaven's sake,' I stammered, 'what have I done, Barbara?' I simply couldn't understand her at all. She turned away from me furiously but not before I saw the suspicion of tears in her eyes.

'Oh, leave me alone!'

There was a pause for a moment or two while I thought of any little thing that I might have said or done to offend or upset her other than taking the lead rather abruptly in the city, but I couldn't think of anything. I moved back to where the Doctor was finishing his cup of water and I could see he'd watched the whole performance very closely.

'A little rift in the lute, Chesterton?' he said, beaming at me happily. It wasn't a moment when I appreciated his sense of humour.

'Mind your own business,' I muttered rudely. The Doctor clicked his tongue sympathetically.

'Dear, dear, dear. That's a sullen sort of temper you have there, Chesterton. You'll have to mend it, my boy, if you want to stay friends with everybody, eh?'

I glared at him murderously.

'There are times, Doctor,' I said through my teeth, 'when I could cheerfully pick you up, turn you upside down and drop you on your head. Preferably from the top of a mountain.'

It was so much water off a duck's back for he smiled at me in the most engaging fashion, as if I'd just paid him a compliment.

'Oh, you can work your feelings off on me if you like. It's all right when I'm in a good mood.' He came over to me and patted my shoulder. 'But if I were you, Chesterton,' and he glanced speculatively at Barbara's back and dropped his voice, 'I wouldn't show any feelings at all.'

He stepped back and suddenly in his eyes I noticed a genuine expression of friendship.

'You'd be surprised what happens when you learn to control your emotions, my friend. It's the quickest way to learn the truth.'

'What truth? What are you talking about?'

'My dear fellow, you don't want me to tell you. The whole key to life is discovering things for yourself. What you do with that discovery is what lies on the other side of the door.'

Alydon stepped into our little glade at that moment, otherwise I would have questioned the old man further. I hadn't any idea what was the matter with Barbara and the Doctor hadn't helped me one bit, although he was obviously driving at something.

Alydon said, 'Why did the Daleks kill Temmosus?'

'I'm not absolutely sure,' I replied slowly, 'but I think I have an idea.'

I saw Susan come into the glade with Dyoni and even Barbara forgot her moodiness sufficiently to come nearer and listen to the conversation.

'Why are they against us?' he said quietly. 'We came to them in peace. We offered to work with them. And yet they kill us. Why?'

'I believe it's simply a dislike for the unlike,' I replied.

The Doctor nodded and added, 'There'll never be any sort of treaty or understanding between the Thals and the Daleks as far as I can see, Alydon.'

After a minute, he said wearily, 'You don't see any hope then?'

The Doctor shook his head. 'Not if you sit back and accept the situation. Of course there's hope if you try and change your way of life.'

'That would be impossible.'

'Even if your way of life means death?' asked the Doctor.

'Even then.'

Dyoni stepped forward and there was no disguising the coldness in her face.

'None of you understands our principles. It is not simply that we are against fighting. Making war is totally alien to us. This planet Skaro is proof enough of what happens when there is war.'

The Doctor bristled. He stepped up to her and pointed a long finger at her.

'This planet, Madam,' he said sharply, 'is an illustration of the evils of stupidity and ignorance. I'm no advocate of human conflict. I have seen splendid races destroyed; brilliant cultures lost beyond recall; marvellous cities in dust and rubble, where beauty and grace flourished. But terrible though it may be, one must sometimes commit an offence in order to stamp out the greater evil. I say to you, fight! Struggle to hold on to life. Protect the weakest of you and honour the eldest. Provide for the girls and the mothers. Teach the children.'

Alydon said, 'All these things we mean to do.'

'That is precisely what you will fail to do,' replied the Doctor, 'if you give in to the Daleks.'

Alydon and Dyoni looked at each other. It was not a look of indecision, merely a mutual bewilderment at not being able to make us understand their point of view. The Doctor waved his hands hopelessly and gave a sigh.

'It's of no consequence to us anyway. We're leaving.'

Alydon gave a short bow and took Dyoni's arm. They disappeared among the trees again. The Doctor frowned at me.

'Have you ever known such contrary people, Chesterton? Here they have the opportunity to rebuild this world and make something out of it and all they want to do is sit back and give in.'

He patted his pockets absent-mindedly.

'But they do have a point of view?' Barbara said.

'Oh, yes,' he replied, 'I see that. It just happens to be the wrong one.'

He delved his hands into his trouser pockets and started searching in the inside pockets of his tail-coat.

'I don't think they even know how to fight,' said Susan. 'I was talking to one of them who told me his name was Kristas. He was looking after a long metal canister and I asked him what was in it. It's their history.'

The Doctor stopped searching for a moment and looked over his spectacles at her.

'Really, my child? I wouldn't mind having a look.'

'I asked him what would happen if anyone came along to steal it,' Susan went on.

'"Who'd want to steal it," Kristas replied, so I suggested that one of us might, if we were evil people. And that, if we wanted it badly enough, we might possibly kill him to steal it.

'"Kill me?" he said in astonishment. "You wouldn't have to kill me. I'd give you the canister."'

Susan folded her arms and leant against a tree. Some of the bark disintegrated and formed a little white cloud and settled on the ground at her feet.

'Well, I persisted because I wanted to find out how they thought about things. So I asked him what would happen if we stole it and silenced him. Do you know, Mr Chesterton, all he did was shrug and say, "Then I would die, wouldn't I?"'

The Doctor began exploring his pockets again and I noticed a worried frown on his face.

Barbara said, 'Are we going back into the Ship, Doctor?'

He nodded in an abstracted sort of way, then suddenly his face cleared. He walked over to me and held out his hand.

'Give me the fluid link, Chesterton, will you?'

I stared at him. He tapped his thumb on top of his fingers impatiently.

'Come on, man. I gave it to you in that little room where all those barometric machines were.'

'You certainly did no such thing.'

'But I must have done. You remember, I was ill and then you…' He stopped and half turned away. 'No, that's right. I didn't. I had it, didn't I? I can't have dropped it because there's a button flap over the pocket.'

He felt round at his hip and I saw a startled look across his face. He pulled his coat aside and quite clearly I could see where the button and the flap of his pocket had been neatly cut away.

Nobody said anything for quite a while, although we were all thinking the same thing. It was left to the Doctor to mutter the answer we were all afraid to admit.

'The Daleks have taken the fluid link. It's down there, somewhere in the city!'

Practically all the rest of that day we spent talking and arguing with the Thals. The Doctor wanted to form them into an army and invade the city but Barbara was against this. If they did fight, she said – and she admitted that the Daleks would hunt them down and exterminate them if they didn't – then they must do so of their own volition.

So we were a camp divided. The Doctor and I took one view and Barbara and Susan took another.

The end was the same but it was the means to that end that set us quarrelling among ourselves. The Thals were frankly bewildered. It was quite clear that they simply had no conception of what fighting meant. They seemed to understand words like bravery and courage and only a fool would have called them cowards, but actual hostility was so strange to them it was like trying to explain what colour means to a blind man.

I tried everything I knew, ending finally with what I was sure would not only explain what we were getting at but illustrate forcefully the physical strength that was inside them. The male Thals were all powerful, muscular men with splendid physiques and I came across the idea when I talked to Ganatus about physical fitness. He explained to me that they had several contests they engaged in, such as racing against each other and jumping. I decided to organize a boxing match. I picked Ganatus and his brother, Antodus, as the contestants and explained the rules to them. Then I marked out a rough square and appointed Alydon as a 'second' for Ganatus and the Doctor as one for Antodus. I was to be the referee.

'The point of all this,' I started, conscious of the entire race of Thals grouped around to watch the new game, 'is to decide which of you is the stronger and the most agile. I shall award points to the one who is able to hit the other, although you must be fair and only hit the opposing body in an area from above the waist. And further,' I went on, encouraged by the attention both the men were giving me, 'you must only hit the front part of the body or face. I shall penalize the man who boxes badly by hitting a foul blow. We shall have three rounds and there will be rests between each round.'

The two men nodded thoughtfully and then Ganatus frowned.

'I have a question. What is the ultimate result?'

'To see which of you is the stronger.'

'And the most agile,' added Ganatus, 'yes, I remember you said that. But I can pick Antodus up or he can pick me up to prove the first. And a running race would decide the second.'

'But here you prove which of you can knock the other man down,' I explained patiently.

Antodus said, 'Why should I wish to knock my brother down?'

'Why should you want to win a running race?' I replied, having expected them to ask such questions. My answer seemed to satisfy them, for they faced each other and when I asked them if they were ready they smiled at me and said they were.

They just stood in front of each other with their hands by their sides.

'You may score the first point,' said Ganatus.

Antodus lifted his hand and tapped his brother on the chest lightly. The crowd applauded politely and the two men stepped back proudly and gazed at me for some mark of pleasure. I saw Susan giggling behind her hand and frowned at her. Then I took the two men to one side.

'Look, you aren't getting the idea right. When I say hit, I mean hit hard. And Ganatus, when your brother goes to hit you, you must defend yourself.'

'But I have scored the point,' protested Antodus.

'Yes, and I have my turn to come,' added his brother. I ran a hand through my hair, trying to avoid looking at the Doctor who was holding his sides with laughter. 'Why didn't they realize how important it was?' I asked myself furiously. I decided to have one last try.

'Ganatus, you fight me. Now watch. Hold your hands up in

front of your body and your face, like this. Clench your fists, man! That's right.'

Ganatus was game enough and his brother stood back and watched us carefully. I squared up to him keeping my right near my face and probing out with my left, my chin well tucked down. Ganatus did his best to copy me but it was a pretty amateurish effort. Still, it was a beginning.

'All right, Ganatus, now shoot your right fist forward and hit me with it. When I count three. Remember, hit me as hard as you can. Right – one... two... three!'

Ganatus thrust out his arm about six feet away from me and then jumped at me, using his arm like a lance. I was so surprised by this, I ducked down and he sailed over my shoulder and landed in a heap on the floor. There was a tremendous roar of laughter from the Doctor and he fell over backwards into the crowd, who forgot their politeness and shouted with delight. Ganatus jumped to his feet and ran over and congratulated me.

'Ah, now I see,' he exclaimed, his eyes alight with pleasure and admiration. 'Agile and strong, you avoid me and bring me down as well.'

I nodded dumbly and accepted the applause they gave me and the hearty slaps on the back and walked away. I passed the Doctor, who was sitting on the ground with tears streaming out of his eyes and holding his chest with the pain of too much laughing.

'Magnificent, Chesterton, absolutely magnificent,' he gasped, but I didn't answer him.

A cold, dogged fury began to overtake me. Ever since the fateful meeting on Barnes Common I seemed to have been nothing more than a pawn in someone else's game, pushed about here and there or waiting for someone else to make a move. I was sick and tired of it. I wanted to do something to get hold of the problem we were in and swing it around my head somehow. I moved away from the main body, who were now engaged in shouting encouragement at Ganatus and his brother to repeat my success. I spent a little of my fury against one of the white trees and I hit it so hard my fist went deep into the trunk. I felt a touch on my shoulder and I pulled out my hand and turned around to see Alydon and Dyoni standing behind me.

'Do not be upset, my friend,' he said quietly. 'I feel I know what you were trying to show us but you have failed now, as you will always fail. Fighting is not for our people.'

'All right, then, you'll all die. All of you,' I said bitterly. Some of the crowd heard me and began to cluster round us. I saw Barbara in the front watching me.

'Yes, we may all die,' said Dyoni proudly, 'but because there is no other way. How can we do what we don't know how to do.'

'Or what we mustn't do,' added Alydon gently, 'because we know it to be wrong.'

I gripped him by the arm roughly.

'Supposing I was to take your history. That canister that you have guarded so well. You must prize it very highly.'

'Take it where?'

'To the Daleks. They may exchange it for the piece of equipment they stole from us.'

'We hope you will not take it. But, if you desire to do so, no one here will stop you.'

All the Thals were grouped round us and the Doctor and Susan stood beside Barbara. I noticed that there was no laughter on their faces now.

I hated what I was going to have to do but I knew it was the last hope left. I pushed Alydon on the chest with my forefinger so hard that he had to retreat a pace or two. The crowd gave behind him but what interested me most was a certain steely look appearing in his eyes.

'Maybe taking the history canister won't satisfy the Daleks,' I said as unpleasantly as I could. 'Maybe they want one of you to experiment on. They must have vast laboratories underneath their city and you Thals are something of a mystery to them. Perhaps I ought to take one of you.'

The ring of faces around me seemed to set into a watchfulness I had never noticed in the people before. The only movement at all came from Barbara as she suddenly clasped her hands together in front of her. The Doctor's glasses caught the sun and they flashed momentarily. Alydon stared back at me and I knew that what I had said had gone home. I stepped forward and put my hand on Dyoni's wrist.

'This girl. I shall take her to the Daleks.'

There was a sort of sigh from the crowd that might have been disapproval or might have been fear. Still Alydon didn't move or say a word. The girl's face betrayed her horror of what I had suggested but she made no effort to draw back. I turned and started to drag her after me, as Dyoni gave one agonized glance at Alydon.

I heard some heavy footsteps and then I was pulled round by a firm hand on my shoulder. A fist crashed into my jaw and I spun away, breaking a small tree behind me and falling with branches and twigs crumbling and snapping all around me.

As a blow it wasn't a particularly hard one really; nor was it well directed. It had the merit of surprise, even though I was hoping for it. It was almost more of a push than anything else but all I could think of as I fell was that it had been offered by Alydon to stop me from doing something; that just as I had used violence, so had he. I looked up at him towering above me, with one of his arms protectively around Dyoni's shoulders.

I said, 'So there is something you'll fight for.'

111

There was a long silence and then I saw the muscles begin to relax on Alydon's arm and he passed a hand slowly over his eyes as if he were trying to wipe away some thick cobwebs that affected his sight. He allowed Dyoni to lead him away and a minute later that part of the forest was empty as the Thals silently trooped away after them.

For a while I stayed where I was, listening to their movements getting farther and farther away. Susan helped me to my feet and I brushed the debris away from my clothes.

'Well, Chesterton,' murmured the Doctor, 'I feel you have proved something.'

'Has he?' I could see the scorn in Barbara's eyes. 'What have you really done, except play silly, ridiculous games?'

'I've decided that with or without the Thals, I'm going down to that city tomorrow to get the fluid link back,' I said grimly.

'More heroics?' she said. I looked at her levelly.

'No. There just isn't any other way.'

'You're a fool, Ian Chesterton,' she said sharply. 'What can you do against those... those things down there? I forbid you to go.'

'You forbid me!' I echoed. 'We'll see about that.' We looked into each other's eyes for a second or two and there was something in hers that utterly defeated me. Then she turned on her heel and walked away, back in the direction of *Tardis*. The Doctor and Susan had been silent partners to the quarrel, although I knew that Susan was bursting to say something.

'Why is she being so unfair?' she cried out at last. The Doctor patted her arm and started to follow in Barbara's footsteps.

'She isn't being unfair, Susan my dear,' he said quietly. 'Miss Wright is asking questions and that is a different thing entirely.'

'What questions, Grandfather? I don't understand?'

Neither did I for that matter, so I listened as carefully as I could without giving away that I was in any way interested.

'Oh, she knows the answer already. The trouble is she doesn't believe it.'

I saw a look pass between the two of them then Susan glanced at me. She said, 'Oh, I see.'

I didn't know what they were talking about, but there was no way of finding out without going into it and I was determined not to do that. Inside *Tardis*, Barbara was very quiet, as if she regretted what had happened, and I had no wish to prolong the quarrel so we managed to be distantly polite to each other.

I had one setback that didn't help me to sleep that night and that was the discovery that the Doctor carried no armaments of any kind whatsoever on board. When Susan had mentioned this earlier in the cell underneath the city, saying that she had borrowed one of her Grandfather's walking-sticks because it was all there was to defend herself with, I had dismissed this as a lack of knowledge on her part. Obviously, I had thought then, the Doctor wouldn't want her meddling with guns or explosives. It was quite a shock to find that the only destructive thing was a small supply of the everlasting matches I had first seen the Doctor use in the fog on the Common. I had no idea how the Daleks would react to flame but I thought the matches might come in handy and he seemed willing to part with them.

The morning brought a new surprise, however, that put all thoughts of a solo attack on the city to flight. Alydon was waiting for us when we stepped outside the Ship and I saw the two brothers, Ganatus and Antodus, with Dyoni, standing a little way behind him. He walked over and addressed himself directly to me.

'I know exactly what you did and why you did it. I still could not restrain myself. I had to stop you. You were right, I care about life and you have made me realize that I care.'

I put out a hand and gripped his. We crowded round him

and the Doctor beamed at him.

'Well done, young man,' he said approvingly. 'You're not afraid to admit you've learned something. The point is, how to profit by it, eh?'

Alydon nodded. 'For myself, it is simple. I shall go with you to the city. The Thals have elected me to be their leader now that Temmosus is dead. I am going to speak to them and tell them of my decision now. I wish you to accompany me and hear the result.'

We followed him to where the Thals were clustered in their familiar semicircle. I managed to catch Alydon just before he moved into his speaking place before them.

'I do want you to be quite clear about one thing, Alydon,' I said urgently. 'I'm going down to that city whatever happens. What I did yesterday had nothing to do with that at all, except that it gave me the ability to show you the right way for you and your own people.' I put a hand on his shoulder.

'You see, I have to go to the city or else my friends and I will die. I believe the same choice lies before you. But what I want to impress on you, Alydon, is that I am not asking you to sacrifice your people on our behalf. You must believe that.'

He smiled at me slightly then moved to his position in front of the Thals.

'Thals,' he began, 'I have thought over the matter I discussed with you all last night. You have elected me to replace Temmosus, but I cannot speak to you as your leader now. I can only say the words of Alydon and tell you what he thinks and what he is going to do. A part of my mind has been blank all these years and I suspect it is the same with you. I have shut out what I would not accept. Now, I *must* accept it. Which is the greatest responsibility? To live by our principle and not fight? To allow ourselves to be hunted and captured and then exterminated? That is what I have always believed because there seemed to be no other alternative. But I have found a new responsibility, and that is to *exist*. We were born to survive, not to die, and living is a much harder thing to do than dying. I say to myself, why even struggle against the elements? The scorching sun that has ruined our crops and made us travel in search of food? Why not just sit down in that sun for ever until we burn away or die of thirst? I say to myself, why even battle with the soil to grow things? I realize that all life is a struggle.'

I felt Susan's hand touch mine and hold it. Perhaps she felt, as I did, that something new was being born here, some new purpose in the Thals – yet it was a purpose that was as old as time itself.

Alydon looked around the crowd facing him and smiled a little sadly.

'So I say this to you. There is no dishonour in dying but there is a terrible shame in giving up life.'

His words began to take on a new note of confidence and authority and I thought of the speech Temmosus had made just before he had been killed. It seemed to me that the Thals chose their leaders wisely.

'There is food in the City of the Daleks. They have killed Temmosus and others of us. I intend to go there and find some way to make them help us.'

He paused for a moment and folded his arms.

'I do not mean to steal from them,' he said at last, 'although they have stolen life from some of us. But this time, if I am attacked… I shall fight back.'

Ganatus and Antodus stepped forward to his side.

'I speak for my brother and myself,' said Ganatus. 'We shall go with you.'

Then there were shouts of agreement on all sides and the Thals surged forward and surrounded Alydon, the men eagerly competing with each other to join him and bombarding him with questions about his plans and the women asking how they could help. The children jumped and leapt with glee and cried out to be lifted on their mothers' shoulders so that they could see more of Alydon and hear what he was saying.

The Doctor walked past me, delved into his inside pocket and put something to his lips. The shrill blast of a whistle cut through the confusion and the shouting died away into a silence of astonishment. I smiled to myself at the way the Doctor produced his little stage effects, but he never failed to get what he was after. This time it was attention and he was totally rewarded.

'My friends,' he said, and I nearly thought he was going to add 'Romans and Countrymen' his manner was so theatrical, 'an affair of this sort needs an experienced planner, a general.' He paused dramatically and then put one hand over his heart and bowed slightly to them. 'I offer my services.'

And that was how, two hours later, I found myself leading a small party away from the city and down towards that thick belt of vegetation I had glimpsed from the observation roof.

The Doctor's plan was based on a remark made by Ganatus – that he had already explored the lake with his brother and two others before they came to the forest and had found it full of underwater creatures and dangerous reptiles. Two of their number had been lost and the place had been declared impassable. When he was escaping with his brother, however, Ganatus had noticed a number of thick metal pipes running out of the mountains and down into the lake. The Doctor decided that the Daleks had run pipes through the mountain to draw up water and refine it and possibly it provided them with hydro-electric power, too, since he was convinced that the static electricity they employed could not come from any atomic source.

So he decided to split his 'army', as he now called it, into two groups. The larger one to distract the Daleks from the forest and desert area and, at a specified time, invade the city and cause as much trouble as possible. The smaller, which was entrusted to me, to force a way through the mountains. Then at the agreed time they were to attack the Daleks from the rear. It was a perfectly sound plan as far as it went, except that we had no guns of any sort at all. We would have to rely on surprise.

Apart from our lack of weapons, there was one other thing that bothered me. Barbara had insisted on coming with my party. I argued myself blue in the face but it didn't make any difference, she was determined, and eventually I was faced with either refusing to go myself or giving in to her.

So there were six of us. Ganatus and Antodus chose themselves because they had at least some knowledge of the terrain. Then there were two other Thals, Elyon and Kristas, the latter a huge man of nearly seven feet with a pair of jet black eyes that contrasted strangely with his head of yellow hair. Finally, Barbara and me, two people who suddenly had nothing to say to each other and apparently no other bond than the will to live.

It took us over four hours to climb down the slopes from the forest and reach the belt of green vegetation, and from there onwards the going began to get slower and more unpleasant.

Any ordinary jungle would have been enough to tackle but here everything was mutated. Wild flowers were everywhere, four or five heads to a stalk and each containing stripes and dots of different colours. Giant bushes grew out of the sides of trees, the roots of which gave birth to not one but many trunks. The nearer we got to the lake, the greater the mutation was. Worst of all was the weed grass which was twice the height of an average man, each blade as thick as a bamboo cane. Gradually, it closed in around us.

Antodus led the way with the giant Kristas at his elbow,

hacking their way through the undergrowth and forcing a way towards the lake. I followed these two, helping Alydon carry our food supplies and a small round canister that the Thals called their 'fire-box', while Ganatus and Barbara brought up the rear. Occasionally, the roar of some animal would shatter the silence and we would all stop in a vain attempt to work out how far away it was, but there was really no way of judging and certainly we heard no movements anywhere near us. The hard ground we had been travelling over for so long began to give way to soggy, squelchy mud and since we had only had one rest of twenty minutes in the whole journey, I asked Antodus to pick out a fairly dry section so that we could eat and collect our strength.

'Very soon,' he said, speaking over his shoulder, 'we'll be at the edge of the lake. My brother and I found an excellent spot there, a shelf of rock, it's also protected on two sides. We should reach it very soon.'

I passed the news back to Ganatus and Barbara who were about ten yards behind me. Barbara was struggling on without a word of complaint, obviously determined not to be a hindrance, but my anxiety increased. She was breathing heavily now and her face was lined with exhaustion. Ganatus made it appear that he was with her not because she needed help but because he preferred her company, and kept up a stream of amusing conversation as he guided and assisted her. Even so, the strain was telling on her and I breathed a sigh of relief when we broke out of the vegetation and walked alongside the lake towards the shelf of rock Antodus had described. We all threw ourselves down on it gratefully, except Kristas who appeared to have regarded the journey as a short afternoon walk and announced that he would keep watch. Nobody argued with him. Darkness was beginning to close in around us about half an hour later when I got them all together.

'We can't go on any farther now,' I said, 'so I suggest we make ourselves as comfortable as we can here and find those water pipes first thing in the morning.'

'That means circling the lake,' murmured Ganatus. 'We certainly can't cross it.'

Barbara said, 'Couldn't we make a raft? It would be a quicker way.'

'There are things in the lake,' replied Antodus, which disposed of any short cuts. The thought of floating on the top of that lake and finding some reptile out of a sailor's nightmare bobbing up a few feet away made a long circle round the swamp seem pleasant. Elyon, who had elected himself as chef, set up the fire-box, which also gave out a powerful light, and announced that he was taking the water-bags down to the lake.

'You mean we can drink that stuff!' I protested. He produced a capsule of little square tablets.

'After we add one of these. The food,' he went on sadly, 'will not be very exceptional.'

'If it isn't any good,' said Ganatus, 'we'll eat you, my friend.'

'Alive,' growled Kristas.

I grinned at them all, admiring their high spirits, and Elyon disappeared in the direction of the lake.

Antodus said, 'I suggest we take guard duty in rotation.' I immediately agreed and fortunately Barbara was asleep so we were able to work out a rota which would allow her a full night's rest.

Suddenly we heard Elyon's voice from the lake. It floated across the still night air and made us all jump to our feet and strain our eyes in the direction he had taken. It was just one word but it contained all the awareness of impending doom, all the knowledge of approaching death, all the shrillness of a man

119

in absolute dread. It was as if a ghostly hand had strummed its fingers across the taut wires of our nerves.

'Kristas!'

The moment of silence as we all stood there was abruptly broken by Kristas, who was the first to collect his wits. He leapt off the shelf of rock and ran into the blackness of the night. Barbara woke up and I ordered Antodus to stay with her. Ganatus and I followed Kristas.

We found him kneeling beside the lake staring at two of the water-bags which floated on top of the water. He looked at me and held out his hand silently. He was holding a scrap of Elyon's cloak, a strip about three inches in width and seven or eight inches long. I lit one of the Doctor's matches and we all stared at the piece of material together. One end of it was soaked in blood.

I looked out at the lake but nothing had disturbed its surface, no ripples gave us any sign or answered the horrified questions we asked ourselves.

Elyon was dead and the lake would reveal the secret of his dying only to its next victim.

CHAPTER EIGHT

The Last Despairing Try

The pale light of dawn brought a strange kind of beauty to the swamp. It had been difficult to sleep after what had happened to Elyon but finally the exhaustion of the journey down the mountain from the forest began to tell and one by one we fell into a fitful, uneasy sleep. Even Kristas confessed to me, when he shook me awake to take over the last watch, that his eyelids were heavy.

'I have a strange feeling,' he whispered, careful not to arouse the others, 'of wanting to do something about Elyon's death. I have never known violent death before.'

He stared moodily into the light of the fire-box.

'Oh, there have been accidents. My father was crushed by rocks in a landslide. But these things are a part of life.' He lifted his head and stared at me. 'Do you understand me when I say that what happened to Elyon was a part of death. Evil and monstrous.'

I knew how he felt. There was a part of him that had lain dormant, as with all the Thals, that part that knows adversity and battles against it. I thought about this and other things and after a long silence turned to him to explain what was being born inside him, but he was asleep. I sat there by the fire, watching the way its light gave way to the birth of the sun, wondering what the new day would bring. The swamp appeared to be calm and perfectly innocent, for none of the animal roars disturbed the night and nothing moved. I was grateful for the absence of any type of insects but I did wish there were birds or small tree animals that might have served as a warning of approaching danger.

I woke them up as late as I dared and after a hot drink of Ratanda – a kind of nut the Thals cultivated which, when boiled, produced a very satisfying drink rather like orange tea – we broke camp and began the journey round the lake to where Ganatus said the pipes were situated. This time Antodus carried the fire-box and Kristas and I brought up the rear. I had decided to have Ganatus lead the way with Barbara. Wherever possible I picked up the driest branches I could find until we were all loaded with them.

The hardest decision of all was the route. The swamp itself was passable only by means of the greatest effort. Thick vines the size of young trees were everywhere, twisted together. Giant trees and undergrowth combined with them to make every yard a struggle. On the other hand the vegetation ceased abruptly about twenty feet from the lake and the ground underfoot, although soft and muddy, was comparatively easy going. We could either take three or four times as long hacking our way through the undergrowth but be out of sight or take the quicker way, where all eyes could spot us, and be vulnerable to any attack. Eventually I decided it was worth the risk to take the quicker way, so we proceeded and made good time.

They all questioned me about the brushwood I made them carry, but I wouldn't be drawn. I felt I might be being overcautious and it didn't impose too much hardship on them to bear a few small branches over their shoulders.

The edge of the lake suddenly began to veer and then we came to a few rocks and scrambled over and around them and the pipes came into view. They were enormous metal constructions, piercing right out of the mountains and down into the water. What lifted my spirits was the sight of the dark edge around where they left the mountainside.

'There are caves there,' I told Kristas, 'either natural ones or cut out by the Daleks. How far away do you think we are?'

He considered for a moment.

'Perhaps a mile, but that is direct. It may take us over an hour to reach the base of the mountain.'

At that very moment, the creature reared out of the water. Its very size was enough to dry up my mouth as tons of water cascaded off its scaly back and plunged back into the lake. With a body the thickness of a house, its head seemed to be all teeth and on the short neck I could see two pairs of claws. I knew in an instant they must be there to feed things into the brute's mouth. A gigantic roar echoed out and it started towards us, sending huge ripples all around it and I could see it had six webbed feet on either side of its body, which propelled it forward through the water at a frightening speed.

'Run! Kristas, stay with me. You two! Get Barbara into the undergrowth.'

The two brothers stared at me for a moment.

'Go on!' I shouted at them and they grabbed hold of Barbara and rushed her off.

'Kristas, the brushwood!'

123

We ran over to the little collection the others had dropped and added our own to the pile. The monster was threshing through the water now and seemed to fill the whole sky. I scrabbled in my pocket and found one of the Doctor's everlasting matches, struck it on a rock and, to my intense relief, the wood flared into flame instantly.

Kristas and I picked up the flaming torches and turned just as the head of the monster reached out from the water's edge towards us. A thrill of fear ran through me as I saw one terrible, red eye glaring malevolently at me and the branch nearly dropped out of my nerveless fingers. Kristas was equally dumb-struck. The monster's mouth opened and began to show rows of razor-sharp teeth.

I remembered Elyon. I shouted his name to Kristas and he jumped into action. We both jabbed upwards into the creature's enormous head and then fell over backwards as it squealed out in agony and reared up. One of the torches had gone right into its mouth and lodged there and, as Kristas helped me to my feet, I saw the arms on the neck pulling at the branches in a vain endeavour to dislodge them. Then one of the flames must have reached that terrible eye and a louder and much more horrible bellow rent the air and the monster threshed sideways into the water. A huge spray drenched us and I caught a vision of a giant tail shooting out from beneath the surface, circling in the air and landing with an ear-splitting slap straight across the top of the lake.

We ran after the others without another backward glance and found the three of them waiting for us at the edge of the undergrowth. Tears were running down Barbara's face but there was another look from the two brothers, one very similar to the one that Kristas wore. It was a look of strange excitement and I recognized it instantly and was glad. They knew they were fighting now, that it was possible to stand against what seemed to be the invincible and defeat it. For the first time I felt that they were not simply the survivors of the planet Skaro, eking out a miserable half-existence and shutting their eyes to reality. They were the true heirs ready to earn their inheritance.

We were about to move away when an incredible sight greeted our eyes. The entire surface of the lake erupted as twenty or thirty of the giant monsters shot into view and began to fight for the injured body of the one we had just defeated. Blinded and totally surrounded, it still fought briefly for life but the others must have known it was virtually defenceless and ripped and tore it to shreds before our eyes. Tremendous roars and squeals nearly deafened us and bigger and bigger waves began to crash against the undergrowth. I shouted to Ganatus to move on, content that our enemies were too occupied to care about us.

It took us just over an hour to reach the mountainside and we rested for ten minutes under the shade of the two huge pipes. The sun was violently hot by this time and I examined the pipes, but as a ladder they were useless. Antodus had already singed his trousers against them and I ordered everyone to keep as far away from them as possible. They were soaking up heat and the lake steamed and bubbled where they entered. The pity of it was that there were metal clasps running up the pipe and if they'd been cooler we could have clambered up and into the caves easily.

'If only we'd thought of bringing a rope,' I said bitterly to Ganatus.

'The rock face is smooth,' he admitted, 'but it can be climbed.'

'In this heat? It's twice as bad as it was yesterday.'

He nodded and fell silent.

'We'll just have to wait for nightfall,' I murmured, and he looked at me.

'Night? And those creatures?'

I shrugged irritably and moved away, staring through the pipes at the lake. It was totally calm now and all traces of the battle had disappeared. Barbara touched my arm and handed me a drink of water. It was warm but I was grateful for it. I nodded and turned away, my mind busy with the problem of reaching the caves above us.

'Ian…'

I turned back to her and looked at her straight in the eyes.

'Look, Barbara, just because I was lucky with that… that thing from the lake doesn't mean you have to apologize.' She opened her mouth to speak but I went on quickly: 'I know… there isn't anything to say sorry for. All right! Let's just finish this business and get back to the Ship and the Doctor.'

She said, 'And then what?'

'I don't know. Let's hope he can take us back to Earth again – if you think the world's big enough for the two of us!'

At that moment Kristas appeared carrying a huge creeper over his shoulder which trailed after him like a huge snake.

'We needed some sort of rope,' he said quietly and dumped it down at my feet. I was only half aware that Barbara hadn't looked at him at all but was still staring at me. Then she walked away. Oh, well, I thought, you can't be liked by everybody. I took Kristas's hand and shook it as hard as I could and I suppose it must have felt like a feather caressing a battleship. It was a bit ridiculous anyway. Even at full stretch, my hand couldn't close around the palm of his.

He smiled at me then shaded his eyes and looked upwards at the place where the pipes came out of the mountain.

'One of us must climb up with the creeper,' and he looked at me with a slight twinkle in his eyes. 'I suggest the strongest of us. Either you or me.'

'I don't fancy pulling a great hulk like you up on the side of a mountain. You'll have to go.' He nodded gravely as if there were really any choice at all between us. He could have picked me up and thrown me like a cricket ball if he'd wanted to.

'The trouble is,' I went on, 'the heat, Kristas.'

'Worse trouble at night.'

He picked up the creeper, tested it with his huge hands and began to coil it.

'If one of us – and I'm willing to try – can make the slow climbing journey the others can be brought up with speed.'

'All right, Kristas, if you promise me you'll give up if the sun gets too much.'

There was a short pause as he went on coiling the rope through his left hand and over his shoulder.

He said, 'It's curious how everything we do I now see in terms of a struggle. I did not realize it before. The sun will be a worthy opponent.'

He walked away and started up the mountain. I joined the others and we watched him anxiously. The first hundred and fifty feet or so were easy with plenty of foot- and handholds, but after that the rock face was smoother. I saw him stop at one point, ease off his sandals and hurl them down to us. The sun glistened on his skin and I knew the deadly process was working. Heat and strenuous exercise bringing out the perspiration which promptly dried in the heat, and however toughened the skin surface was the merciless sun would roast and shrivel it, flaking away each successive layer until it burned its way through to the shrinking flesh beneath.

Now Kristas reached the worst part of all. The mountainside suddenly inclined outwards slightly and even a professional mountaineer with hammer and metal supports, ropes and tackle and climbing boots would have taken as much time as he could. But time was the last thing Kristas could spare. He settled himself securely under the great lip of the rock and looked down at us.

'Can you hear me?' he shouted, and I waved my hand. 'There's a piece of rock to one side of me. I'm going to loop the creeper over it.'

'It looks too risky,' I shouted up to him but he started to pay out the creeper until he held the two ends in his right hand. With the other he took the slack end and bracing his back against the rock threw forward. It caught first time and Ganatus and his brother grinned at each other. Barbara stood beside us, shading her face with both hands as she watched. I saw Kristas pulling on the creeper as hard as he could and felt the sweat springing out on the palms of my hands. If Kristas fell there was only one destination and that was the lake spreading out beneath him – the lake with those monsters. I clamped my teeth together and shut out the thought.

He swung away from safety and started to climb up the creeper laboriously. It meant that he had to hold both ends in one hand as he reached upwards with the other and only those huge fingers of his could have done it. A few minutes later his arm wrapped itself round the little knob of rock and he pulled himself up into the entrance of the cave. We all jumped up and waved our arms at him as he unhooked the creeper and pulled it up beside him. His arm appeared briefly in reply and then one end of the creeper snaked down towards us. It was too short by about fifty yards, of course, but we collected together our food and water-bags and the fire-box and began to scramble up the mountain. I chose the last position this time and the two brothers helped Barbara up first. We had one or two tricky moments where the going became smoother but then it was only a short way to reach the end of the creeper that dangled down so temptingly. One by one, Kristas pulled us up on to the ledge.

I stood there with Kristas for a few seconds.

He said, 'I wouldn't mind going for a swim.'

I looked down into the lake with its clear, sun-tinted surface. Now and again I could just catch the movement of some vast shape too deep to disturb the surface.

'One day you will bathe in that lake, my friend. Or your children will. But you'll have to do a lot of fishing first.'

He chuckled and we moved into the blackness of the cave. At least it was cool inside and the fire-box gave us an excellent light. The difficulties began when the pipes we had hoped to use as a guide all the way suddenly plunged straight into a wall, whereas the cave itself bent to the right. We had no alternative but to follow the cave, but I began to worry about changing direction so sharply and said as much to Antodus.

'I suppose we all hoped that the Daleks had cut a way through the mountain,' he replied, 'but it's becoming obvious that these are natural caves.'

We suddenly entered a small chamber and found we had three ways from which to choose. I counted my supply of the Doctor's matches and found I had four left. I gave one each to Barbara, Ganatus and Kristas.

'Antodus, you take the fire-box and you and Kristas take the right hand.' They nodded and moved off and I lit a match.

'Barbara and I will try the centre,' said Ganatus. He lit his match and started off. Barbara and I looked at each other briefly.

'We'll all meet back here and report progress,' I murmured. She nodded briefly and followed him.

The left-hand mouth lasted for about twenty paces then began to close in. Finally it came to an end, so there was nothing else for it but to go back to the starting place.

I sat there for a few minutes, wondering whether I ought not to follow one of the other pairs, when Kristas appeared and his account was very similar to mine: a narrowing passage which ended in a blank wall of rock. We collected the creeper and provisions and followed Barbara and Ganatus.

This was much more promising at first, developing from a tunnel just high enough to walk in (Kristas had to move along bent double) into a broad channel about twenty feet wide and too high for us to estimate.

Suddenly we heard the sound of falling rocks ahead of us and Barbara's voice calling out. We started to run up the tunnel towards her. The light of the fire-box picked her up hurrying towards us and I moved on ahead of the others.

'It's Ganatus,' she sobbed. 'He's fallen and both our matches are lost.'

'It's all right, Barbara,' I said gently. 'Show us where.'

She led the way forward and the tunnel began to narrow down until the familiar blank wall of rock began to appear before us. Barbara turned sharply to her right and squeezed herself through a slim little crevice.

'Through here. He said he'd found something and then his foot must have slipped. I tried to catch him but then we both dropped the matches and I couldn't see any more.'

I squeezed in after her, wondering how Kristas was ever going to get through, and Antodus passed me the fire-box. I saw a wide fissure, pushed my head through it and held out my hand with the lighted match as far as I could. I was looking into an enormous chamber about twenty feet from its floor level and there was another small glow beneath me. It was Ganatus who was just in the process of sitting up. Beside him was one of the matches.

'Are you all right?' I shouted. He looked up and rubbed his shoulder.

'Yes. Lucky I didn't break anything. At least, I don't think I have.'

He picked up the match and got to his feet.

'Hang on a moment and I'll pass the creeper down.'

'I think it would be better if you all came down with me,' he answered. I considered for a moment then mentally agreed. The chamber looked as if it had possibilities.

The hardest part was just as I'd thought it would be, getting Kristas through the little crevice. Eventually we did, with much pushing from Antodus on his side and pulling from Barbara and me. Then Kristas held the creeper while we all lowered ourselves to the floor of the cavern and finally he jumped down beside us. Twenty feet or so was child's play to him.

I had now lost my sense of direction completely. It seemed to me that we had been turning right all the time and I was terrified that we would find ourselves back where we started again. It was with immense relief that I found the cavern began to bend away to the left. Ganatus and I were leading at this point and as we moved out into a short passage we nearly fell into a chasm that appeared at our feet. We set the fire-box down and Ganatus sat with his feet over the edge.

'There's a ledge on the other side,' he murmured.

'How about going down and up the other side?'

He picked up a piece of rock and let it fall. The wait seemed eternal and when we did hear the rock hit something it wasn't reassuring. It was a loud splash and none of us fancied any deep diving at this stage of the game.

'We'll just have to jump it,' I sighed. 'Well, at least we've got the creeper.'

'Yes,' he replied, 'you can throw it over to me when I'm on the other side.'

'You,' I said definitely, 'can throw it over to me.'

Barbara brought us each a cup of water and some of the Doctor's compressed fruit and we all chewed silently.

'Of course,' murmured Kristas, 'you could let me go first.'

'I've no way of knowing how firm that ledge is,' I answered.

131

I drank the last of the water in my cup and got to my feet. 'Let me have as good a run as possible. Antodus, you're in charge of the lighting arrangement. Hold the fire-box up as high as you can.'

He nodded and moved to the left edge of our side, holding up the fire-box. I examined the ledge and searched above it for any handholds. There didn't seem to be much help there. The ledge itself was about a foot wide and I could see that it continued on to the left then disappeared round a corner. I walked back along the passage, braced myself and ran back past them all and jumped. I over-jumped it slightly and the side of my right knee cracked against the rock. I nearly rebounded backwards, but my feet found the ledge firm enough and I scrabbled around desperately with my hands, just catching on to a jutting piece of stone that saved me. I shook my head and told my nerves to settle down.

'Throw over the creeper, Kristas.' I leaned against the wall and caught it easily. I passed one end of it round my waist then threw the other end back.

'Kristas, we'll have Barbara over next. Hold the creeper round your waist and she can cross hand over hand.'

I wiped my hands carefully on my trousers, suddenly aware of how torn they were. Barbara moved up beside Kristas and looked down into the chasm.

'We won't drop you,' I heard him say gently and she gave him a tight little smile. Then she sat on the edge of the chasm, gripped the creeper above her head and started to swing over. Hand over hand she came, as if she had done it all her life, and when she was a yard away she pulled over her legs and rested them on the ledge and levered herself upwards. I caught her round the waist and pulled her beside me thankfully. Then I felt the muscles tightening in her back and she moved away from me. Isn't there enough to do, I thought angrily, without all this ridiculous hatred.

'There isn't any need to make it quite so obvious,' I breathed furiously. She didn't say a word and as her face gleamed whitely with only the pale glow from the fire-box to illuminate it, I wasn't sure whether there was a smile on her face or not. A sick fury made me press my lips together and it didn't help when I heard a bellow of laughter from the other side of the chasm.

'What is it,' I called out sharply.

'We're just trying to decide,' chuckled Ganatus, 'whether you really want us to cross over or not.'

After the silence, I said, 'Rope coming over,' and their laughter died away. I suppose they were afraid they had offended me or something. Perhaps they thought my sense of humour was a little on the weak side but I didn't feel like explaining.

Personal thoughts were rubbed out as one by one the others made the crossing. Antodus came next, after handing over the fire-box to his brother and then, as soon as he had a firm foothold, Ganatus threw it to him and made his way over. Kristas, let me draw in the creeper and without taking any sort of run at all simply leapt off and landed lightly beside me.

'What we should have done,' I said seriously to him, 'was lay you across the chasm and walk over.' I had recovered my temper at the successful way we had beaten the obstacle and besides I wanted to make up for being so surly with them.

'We might have tried that,' Kristas replied, 'but then somebody might have trodden on my head.'

'They wouldn't have hurt their feet very much.'

He grinned at me and took the fire-box from Antodus.

'All right, Ganatus, you lead on with Barbara. You follow,' I said to Kristas, 'and let's hope we find the pipes again soon.'

They disappeared round the bend in the rock and I heard Ganatus call out that the ledge was widening out. I hitched the creeper over my shoulder more securely and beckoned with my head to Antodus. Kristas had turned the corner with the fire-box so we both lit the last of the everlasting matches and started to follow.

I was just going to turn the corner when Antodus stumbled over his feet and his hand clutched at my shoulder. The creeper unwound and I grabbed at it and pushed myself against the rock, filled with a fear of falling. He tried to regain his balance but failed and just as I twisted to catch hold of him he hung suspended for a second then fell over the edge, his fingers just gripping hold of one end of the creeper.

'Hold on to it!' I cried as it snaked away, pulling at one of my ankles and nearly taking me over the edge as well. I slid down on one side as Antodus screamed out for help and I realized, with a dreadful shock, that it was the first time I had ever known one of our companions admit to any sort of fear at all.

'Kristas!' I shouted and struggled to get a better hold on the creeper. Another yard or so of it slid through my hands and I tried digging my nails into it. I felt one of my feet slipping over the side of the ledge. I daren't let go of the creeper and yet I knew I had to stop the way my body was being inched towards the gaping hole of the chasm. Of course I'd had to drop the match and the pitch blackness didn't help.

'Ganatus! Kristas!' I shouted again and I heard their voices answering me. The rope began to swing, dragging me nearer to destruction.

'Try and get a foothold, Antodus!'

His voice reached up at me from the darkness beneath.

'My hands are slipping. Can't… hold… on.'

Suddenly light appeared as Kristas and Ganatus came around the corner, the former holding up the fire-box.

'Pass the rope under your arm if you can,' I called out. Ganatus edged his way nearer to me and was just about to help me back when the creeper gave a jerk and at the same time there was a long, drawn-out scream and I tumbled backwards. Ganatus knelt beside me and hauled in the creeper unbelievingly. He leaned over the edge and called out his brother's name and just at that moment we all heard the splash as the body hit the water and the beginnings of another scream was cut off almost as soon as it began. There was a second or two's silence then a terrible threshing began, a noise much louder than one man's desperate struggle for life could have made and, as if we needed any confirmation, the terrible screech of some water creature echoed and re-echoed about us. We all waited there in absolute horror as the sounds began to die down and finally there was a little series of splashes and everything became quiet. Ganatus was lying full length along the wider part of the ledge now and trying to stare through the pitch blackness beneath him.

'Antodus!' he called out and when there was no reply he shouted the name again and again. I looked up at Kristas and then at Barbara who had followed them back and now leaned against the rock wall. Her whole body was shivering and her lips were drawn back in tragedy and horror. Eventually Ganatus gave up and buried his face in his hands and sobbed, his whole body racked with emotion. I stared ahead of me dumbly, all purpose gone, despair bringing out all the weakness of my muscles and joints that determination had forced me to forget. It was Kristas who took command and he lifted Ganatus up and told Barbara to carry the fire-box ahead of us. He nudged my shoulder with his foot and I got to my feet silently and followed him.

Ten minutes later the ledge broadened a little more and made an abrupt turn to the left. The chasm ended and we were travelling along a rock passage about seven feet wide and ten feet high. There was no conversation between us, just a dogged sort of persistence. Kristas helped Ganatus to move off and we tramped on with feet like lead, all sharing the same memory of the horrible way Antodus had died.

Again the passage turned to the left and we all stopped.

Ahead of us was a wall of rock! I ran my hands over it, scraping off some of the skin from my fingers, but it was no good. The journey was over and I knew what it was like to have the real taste of failure in my mouth.

CHAPTER NINE

The End of the Power

I don't know how long we lay in that little corridor of rock. The numbing shock of the death of Antodus, coupled with the black despair of defeat when the blank wall appeared to end our progress drained every bit of reserve energy away and left us all listless and without hope. At first Kristas had retraced our steps and gone back to the chasm where the tragedy had occurred to see if there was any other way, but eventually even he gave up and slumped down beside us, his great head bowed low over his chest. Barbara had tried to comfort Ganatus as much as she could but he never replied once and just lay on the ground with his head turned away.

My brain refused to work. I was like a man half asleep and half awake, caught in a kind of no-man's-land where the best course seemed to be indecision and inactivity.

It was the fire-box that saved us. We might have sat there for many more hours until hunger and thirst made us reach out for food and water but all of a sudden the light began to flicker. I saw Kristas raise his head and turn it towards the fire-box and I moved over on my hands and knees slowly towards him.

'We'll have to go back,' he muttered. 'We'll never cross that chasm again without light.'

'How long will it last now?'

'I can only think some water must have splashed into it when we were beside the lake and those monsters were fighting,' he said slowly. 'The cells are supposed to re-charge themselves with their own light and heat. Normally, they only need overhauling every four or five years.'

'You'd better turn it off now.'

I searched in my pockets but all the matches the Doctor had given me were gone, too. Kristas picked up the fire-box and fiddled with some switches underneath it. The light died away. He started to lay it down again and then his hands slowed and stopped, so that he held the contraption several inches from the floor. I saw his face turn and look at me and Barbara bent forward, too, her eyes alert.

'Where is the light coming from?' she whispered.

A strange, excited feeling ran through the whole of my body. It was true! There was a glow from somewhere above us. I jumped up to my feet and located it, about twenty feet to the left of the blank wall.

'Get me up on your shoulders, Kristas!'

The giant bent down and Barbara helped me clamber up. Almost at once I found a cleft in the rock which enabled me to climb even higher. I found I was looking through a hole about six feet in circumference.

I turned back to the others below me.

'I'm going through,' I told them and they must have heard something in my voice. Even Ganatus got to his feet and stared up at me. I edged myself into the hole and started to lever myself forward with my hands and knees. The hole lasted about twenty feet then began to dip downwards and widen out. Beneath me I saw another rock chamber and I nearly laughed with pleasure because on the floor of it ran two metal pipes. I knew they were the ones from the lake. I followed them with my eyes and they disappeared again through another wall, but there was an arch between them and it was open! Through it a strong, white light shone and on the other side of it I could just see the edge of some metal flooring.

I couldn't wait to scramble back and tell them the news.

Kristas was the last to make the journey and he was covered with little cuts and grazes when he finally dropped to the floor the other side. He grinned at me ruefully.

'My size does have its drawbacks.' I slapped him on the back and we crept forward silently to the archway and peered through it.

We were looking into a vast metal room about a hundred feet in height and about twice as long. The width of it was only about twenty feet and spaced at intervals in the floor near the side walls were little platforms that raised and lowered themselves at the press of a switch. Kristas accidentally found this out when he sat down on one to take a small piece of stone out of his leg and was suddenly taken up towards the ceiling. His hands searched round the platform and found a switch and he descended again slowly. The reason for the platforms was obvious because the walls were covered with dials of all shapes and sizes right up to the ceiling. The twin metal pipes themselves each entered a huge boiler shaped affair and on the other side the water was channelled into hundreds of smaller pipes. These pipes ran away to the side walls to connect up to the dials.

'They must drink some of the water,' said Ganatus, 'but most of it seems to be turned into pressure of some sort. See how some of these needles are spinning round in the dials. They must be creating electricity...'

Barbara and Kristas had gone off to explore the other end of the room and I measured up Ganatus in my mind. He was pale now and his eyes had darkness in them but there was a resolve about the set of his lips and purpose enough in the way he held himself.

'We're going on with this, Ganatus,' I said quietly. His eyes looked into mine briefly then moved away over my shoulder.

'Did you think I would give up?'

'I just know that there might not seem to be any purpose in your brother's death. You and I and the others have to make sure there is one. He mustn't have died in vain.'

'No,' agreed Ganatus firmly.

Kristas came marching towards us.

'There's a door and a corridor at the other end. Barbara says she can see a lift.'

'Well, what are we to do? Is there any way we can put this place out of action?' I looked at my watch, mercifully undamaged. 'We're not really due to meet Alydon and the Doctor for another four hours.'

'If we do break anything,' said Ganatus, 'the Daleks will start swarming down here and we might be driven back into the mountain caves again.'

Barbara suddenly ran towards us.

'I can hear alarm bells ringing and announcements going on,' she cried, 'but the words aren't clear.'

With one accord we raced over to the door and along the corridor to the lift. The sound of alarm bells increased and I could hear the voice too; it was above us somewhere and full of urgency.

'Up in the lift,' I ordered and we tumbled into it. I pressed a low button so that we progressed upwards one floor only. The bells were louder now and as soon as the lift stopped and we stepped out into the little ante-chamber that separated all the lifts from the corridors the voice became distinct.

'Emergency!' it grated out. 'The Thals are entering the city. Emergency!'

Then I saw the door in front of us begin to slide sideways and just caught the lowest edge of a Dalek.

'Get back,' I shouted and we fell into the lift again. I jabbed at a button wildly and the lift began to move upwards just as the Dalek slid into the ante-chamber.

'Why have they come earlier?' asked Ganatus but the lift stopped again and this time the door to the corridor was open. I motioned them all to stay where they were and edged across and peered out. The corridor was deserted. I nearly jumped when the voice over the tannoy system broke out again.

'Emergency! Thals are reported to have been seen on level twenty-nine.' That was the one we'd just left. We had escaped from there and risen eight floors so we must be on level twenty-one.

'Report to Master Room when Thals are captured,' the voice continued in its deadly monotone. Then there was a pause and I thought the message had ended. I was just turning away when the voice began again. 'Wait!' it ordered. I waited a few seconds more and it suddenly occurred to me that whoever was doing the announcements was referring to someone else for fresh orders. As if in confirmation the voice spoke again.

'Orders are changed. Do not capture, repeat do not capture Thals. Exterminate. Repeat… exterminate.'

I went back slowly to the others. A master room. A voice that was receiving orders. At last we had a goal. We had to find that Master Room and destroy it.

'We never imagined that they had a leader,' said Ganatus when I told them what had happened.

'Neither did I, I thought they were all equal. I'm beginning to suspect that there *is* someone in charge of them, directing their operations.'

'The point is,' said Barbara, 'where is the Master Room?'

I waved them all back into the lift and pressed a button that would take us up to the tenth level.

'We don't even know if this room is in this particular building,' I explained. 'We'll just have to search round for it.'

The lift stopped once again and we moved out of the ante-chamber cautiously and crossed the corridor. I waved my hand over a wall-bulb and we walked into a small room opposite. The light in it hurt my eyes and I screwed them up and saw that the entire area of the floor, except for two feet all round was taken up by a glass case under which I could see thousands of little green shoots. The heat in the room was terrific and I knew we couldn't stay there much longer.

'Artificial sunlight,' breathed Barbara. 'Don't you see, Ian – that's how they grew things.'

Ganatus suddenly hissed at us from his position at the doorway.

'I can hear something in the corridor.'

We all pressed against the wall. Ganatus swung back next to me and bent his head close to mine.

'Daleks!'

The glass case made a perfect mirror and reflected in the side facing the open door I saw at least twenty Daleks moving smoothly past us. We waited a few seconds after the last one had disappeared then Ganatus peered out again and signalled the all-clear. The Dalek's voice arrested us once again.

'Attention! The operation is due to commence. Daleks will exterminate all Thals in this building.'

I frowned at the others.

'What operation?'

'Level six must be kept clear until the operation is completed,' the voice continued.

'Six!' Barbara said excitedly. 'Could that be where the Master Room is?'

Ganatus signalled silence again with a finger to his lips. I heard a soft scrape out in the corridor. Ganatus clenched his fist and as something began to emerge he leapt out into the corridor. Kristas and I followed in a flash and found him picking himself up. Another man was also struggling to his feet and I went to him and pulled him up delightedly. It was Alydon.

143

We decided to get away from the brightly-lit room and a few yards down the corridor we found the very place, a similar sort of artificial sun room but lit only dimly. The glass case in the centre of the floor was very much smaller this time and nothing grew out of the earth. But there were other things that made me narrow my eyes thoughtfully. The Daleks obviously used this room as a kind of store for implements because there were orderly stacks of long metal rods dotted about. Each stack had different attachments; some had hooks, others small magnets, but it was when I saw a pile that had a sucker-like end that I realized that the Daleks must be able to replace the rods they carried with other types when they were working on different kinds of jobs.

'Anyway,' I said to Kristas, 'we can use some of these as weapons.' I turned to Alydon, who had been hearing the story of our adventures from Ganatus and Barbara. He took the news of the deaths of Elyon and Antodus gravely.

'It seems we have both had our share of misfortune,' he murmured.

'Why? And what's made you invade the city earlier than we agreed?'

'The Doctor and Susan have been captured.'

I stared at him in horror. Barbara gripped his wrist.

'How?' she gasped.

'He had a theory that the Daleks covered their city with mechanical eyes and ears. Radio and television waves he said. I didn't understand too clearly but we agreed to follow his plans. He brought out some shiny metal plates from his travelling machine. *Tardis*, I think he calls it.'

I nodded impatiently.

'Anyway, we shone these towards the city, catching the rays of the sun. This, he said, was to blind the eyes of the city. Then he and Susan and my cousin Gurna went down there.

The Doctor said he had a way to immobilize the radio waves, so that we could enter the city undetected. Gurna came back alone and said we had to invade at once because the Doctor had discovered that the Daleks were planning to explode a bomb in the atmosphere above the city and poison the air. As Gurna reached the desert he happened to look back.'

He gazed around at all of us sadly.

'Well, go on, man!' I demanded.

'Gurna saw the Doctor and Susan surrounded by a ring of Daleks. There was nothing he could do. He just had to stand there watching them being led away.'

'They weren't killed, then?'

He shook his head but I saw in his face that he didn't think they could be alive.

'Now we know what the voice was talking about when it mentioned the "operation",' I said grimly. 'Due to start at any moment. It's the bomb!'

I ran over to one of the stacks of rods and scattered them on the floor. They were the ones with hooks on one end.

'Grab one of these and follow me,' I yelled. They each picked one up and we hurried out into the corridor. There was no caution now and I felt happier with something in my hands. Puny though it was, it was better than nothing. I knew we would be helpless in a long-range battle but I felt we could give a good account of ourselves in any close work. The corridor was a long one and I took hold of Kristas's arm.

'Kristas,' I said. 'I'm giving you a job to do. Guard Barbara. Don't leave her side.'

He nodded reassuringly.

'I will watch over her. I know what she means to you.'

Was he right? Surely I was merely protecting the weakest of our party. I pushed it out of my mind as Ganatus pointed to a box on the wall. I recognized it as similar to the one the

Doctor had smashed in the cell. It had a perfect view of us. I raised up the metal rod and smashed the box right in the middle and it sagged out of the wall. Immediately a chorus of alarm bells started up and the same metallic voice boomed along the corridor.

'Emergency! Thals have been detected on level ten. Close off intersections… close off intersections immediately.'

'There's a lift down here,' called Alydon and then I saw that behind me a whole series of metal doors were beginning to slide downwards.

'How far ahead?' I snapped and hurried on. Kristas suddenly bounded past me and pushed at one of the doors that was trying to cut off our advance. He slowed it a little but couldn't stop its progress. Barbara literally dived past him and ran on ahead.

'One more before the lift,' she screamed out but by this time Kristas was on his knees. We all put our shoulders into holding the door and must have damaged the mechanism because it stopped altogether.

'Ganatus,' I gasped, 'get through and help Barbara. We must get to that lift!'

He squeezed himself between our legs and disappeared. Immediately he was on the other side I heard him urging us to hurry and I forced myself through.

I saw Barbara on her hands and knees holding up the last door. Ganatus helped her but still the door moved downwards gradually, like a guillotine in slow motion. I flung myself forward and managed to get my back underneath it. A high whine began to fill the air as the power of the door was increased but luckily Kristas and Alydon arrived and again we managed to stop the door and scramble through. It fell behind us with a reverberating clang as I pulled Alydon through and we rushed into the lift.

'Some of us managed to get into this building,' Alydon told

us as the lift began to move up, 'but two of my men were cut down in the hall below. Others are trapped in other buildings. I'm afraid we may have lost several.'

I set my mind grimly against any thought of sympathy or pity. We had to smash that Master Room somehow and then we had to find the Doctor and Susan. There wasn't time for tears. That would be for later.

The lift bumped to a gentle stop and we crept out and peered down the corridor. Level six was different from the others because a short way down the left-hand turn I could see a huge archway. I caught a glimpse of Daleks gliding about swiftly within.

I knew instinctively that this was the heart of the City of the Daleks, their Master Room. If we could put it out of action I felt we might just have a chance. At least, I reflected grimly, we'd give a good account of ourselves.

I turned to Alydon.

'Down below we found a kind of hydro-electric plant. Where they turn the water from the lake into power. Ganatus will show you. I want you both to go down there and smash it up. Break the dials, destroy as much as you can.'

'But you'll need us here,' objected Ganatus.

'Don't argue. There isn't time. When you've done that, find as many Thals as you can and bring them up here.'

'Please, Ganatus, do as Ian says,' Barbara said. 'It's the best way.'

If I was surprised at this unexpected support, I didn't show it.

'We've followed you so far,' said Ganatus simply. 'It would be wrong to argue now.'

He stepped back into the lift with the reluctant Alydon and pressed one of the switches. The two of them sank out of sight. I turned to the other two.

'Now listen to me. This isn't, going to be pleasant. If I'm right, this is where they're controlling this bomb. We've got to stop them. There may be dozens of them in there and they're armed. All we have is surprise and greater mobility.'

We pressed ourselves close against the wall as a Dalek hurried by. I peered out again and immediately spotted two doors that faced each other at right angles to the archway. They were obviously little side rooms of some sort but the value of them was that we needn't be caught out in the open corridor. The Dalek that had just passed by might well have gone on some little errand. I didn't fancy being caught in any cross-fire.

'I'll go first. Kristas, you next. Barbara, stay close behind him and keep an eye over your shoulder.'

I stepped out and began to creep up towards what must be the Master Room, searching the walls around me for any more of the viewing boxes that might warn them of our approach, but fortunately there weren't any. I reached the archway and discovered with a shock that it wasn't open as I'd first thought. The way was effectively barred by a plate-glass door, much too thick to break through. It was a setback but I put the problem of how to get into the room aside for the moment and risked a look into the Master Room.

The first thing I saw was a long metal pipe running up to the roof around which four or five Daleks were standing. I could see that they were supervising the tipping of some liquid from a metal container into an oblong box affair that was placed inside the pipe and reached by a glass door. The second thing I saw was a glass Dalek!

He was resting on a kind of dais and his casing was totally made of glass. Inside, I could see the same sort of repulsive creature that the Doctor and I had taken out of the machine and wrapped in the cloak. The Dalek looked totally evil, sitting on a tiny seat with two squat legs not quite reaching the floor. The head was large, and I shuddered at the inhuman bumps where the ears and nose would normally be and the ghastly slit for a mouth. One shrivelled little arm moved about restlessly and the dark-green skin glistened with the same oily substance that had revolted me before.

'Hurry, hurry,' I heard it say and it spoke with a different kind of voice altogether, not like the dull, lifeless monotone of its fellows but more of a dreadful squeaking sound that only just made the words intelligible.

What alerted me was the fact that I could actually hear anything through a thick plate of glass that ought to have made the room soundproof. I looked round for the reason and found it in a metal grille set at floor level on either side of the archway. It was about three feet high from the floor upwards and disappeared into the wall. If it runs along the wall in the side room, I reflected, we can forget the plate-glass door and break through the grille. I opened the side-door and pulled the other two into a little store room full of metal boxes. The grille ran along the wall all right and I beckoned them down. We had a perfect view of the Master Room. Almost immediately, Kristas gripped my shoulder. Barbara and I saw them at the same moment. The Doctor and Susan!

Their arms and legs were clamped on to a wall by huge magnets and they were desperately struggling to free themselves.

'Can you pull this grille out?' I whispered to Kristas. He examined it then nodded confidently.

Barbara said, 'Without any noise?'

'I'll try.'

He put his fingers through the mesh and began to break the strands. I examined the room again and fixed my eyes on a low wall about two feet high which ran round the centre of the room. It was no more than a yard away from us. Here and there it had openings in it, to allow the Daleks to move through into the room proper. It seemed to be some kind of decoration. If it had a purpose we never found out what it was. I could already see how it would be useful to us. I bent close to Barbara and spoke in her ear.

'I think one of us could slip through the grille and crawl round under cover of that little wall and reach the Doctor and Susan. How about it?'

She nodded.

'Good girl. I haven't any idea how strong those magnets are. Do the best you can. Free the legs first where you can work out of sight. Leave the hands until Kristas and I start our diversion.'

'Be very careful, Ian,' Barbara whispered. Kristas had made a wide hole in the grille and we helped Barbara through it. She began to worm her way along the wall and fortunately all the Daleks were now in a fever of activity and she was able to inch along without being seen.

The Doctor stopped his struggling and lifted his head up.

'Stop this senseless slaughter,' he bellowed.

I saw the glass Dalek jump to its feet and give a little dance of rage, its one arm waving furiously and banging the inside of the glass,

'Silence!' it squeaked. 'We shall be the people of Skaro. The only people!'

I heard Kristas give a little groan behind me.

'Is that what we fight? That dreadful thing?' he hissed.

'And it is planning to make the air unbreathable,' I whispered grimly. I turned my attention to the Dalek in the glass casing again.

'Why is it not ready?' it was saying. 'We must hurry, I tell you.'

The Daleks around the metal pipe withdrew the container now, holding it with their sucker-rods, and two of them took it out of my eye-line to the right. The others closed the glass door carefully and then moved to the other side of the metal tube with their backs to us and came to rest before an enormous bank of dials and switches. Barbara had slithered right round the little metal wall by this time and both the Doctor and Susan had seen her, although they kept their faces well to the front so as not to give her away. I saw Barbara pull off the magnets from Susan's legs and I tensed my muscles.

'All right, my friend,' I breathed. 'We smash that glass Dalek. Then do as much damage as we can to those dials.'

He gripped his metal rod firmly. There was the slightest smile on his lips that gave me just that extra bit of courage I needed.

We eased through the broken grille, gathered ourselves on the floor and leapt to our feet together. For some reason or other, I shouted out a bellow of defiance and, waving my metal rod over my head, I rushed at the Dalek in the glass casing.

It was pointed towards the bank of dials and I saw its face turn to stare at me in astonishment as I ran up to it. I saw its casing begin to swivel and knew if the gun-stick could point at me in time I was finished. I jumped to one side as it fired past me and the glass plate covering the archway disintegrated and thousands of little bits of glass flew all over the room. I swung the metal rod high over my head and down and the glass shattered. The thing inside gave the most terrifying screech that made my heart thump against my breast and I saw it slipping over the broken glass and lie wriggling on the floor. Kristas used the metal pipe as a cover and hurled his rod straight at the dials. The Daleks in front of it had swung round at the sound of the death-throes of their leader and the metal rod crashed over their heads.

Immediately there was a tremendous surge of movement as two of the Daleks fired their gun-sticks at me. I dived away, bruising my shoulder on the ground. The blue, sparkling flames bit across the room and melted the wall behind where I had been standing.

Barbara had freed both Susan and the Doctor and was just hurrying them to the archway when it was filled with a dozen Thals led by Ganatus. They poured into the chamber and two of them fell immediately, cut down by the Dalek guns. I saw Kristas get behind one of the Daleks and lift it right off the ground and throw it straight at two others just as they fired. There was a colossal explosion which knocked Kristas backwards, sliding him along the floor towards me. He shook his head once and then picked up a metal canister from the floor near him and smashed in the top of another Dalek with it. I watched Ganatus jump on the back of a Dalek and be carried half across the room until it swivelled round suddenly and threw him off. A blue flame sped out from its gun and just caught the top of his shoulder and Ganatus fell with a groan.

I was busy at the metal pipe in the centre of the room. I could see a hundred wires leading to the oblong metal box inside and I pulled two of them away. A sixth sense warned me of danger and I fell sideways as a Dalek's sucker-stick clanged sideways against the pipe in an effort to crush me. I could see there was just a fingerhold at the bottom of the casing and before it could move any more, I put my hands under it and toppled it over on one side. Another Thal was pinned to the wall on my right and I could see the Dalek sucker-stick embedded in the man's stomach. Then the awful blue flame crackled from its gun-stick and the Thal shivered and collapsed in a smoking heap on the ground.

At that moment all the lights in the room died and at the same time there came the sound of failing engine noises, a gradual whirring down. Kristas was hammering in the top of another Dalek but he stepped back in surprise as all its rods shot upwards into the air. There was a dim light coming from somewhere and I realized that the lighting had only diminished, it hadn't gone out totally. About eighty per cent of the power had failed. I felt a hand helping me to my feet and it was the Doctor, who handed me one of his everlasting matches. He'd obviously distributed them around the room for nine or ten of them were struck almost at the same time. The surviving Daleks were moving again but slowly now and I could see that their rods were beginning to fall downwards. From inside each one I began to hear a kind of moaning sound. It became louder and louder and Susan put her hands over her ears.

'Have you dismantled that bomb, Chesterton,' the Doctor demanded.

'I don't know,' I replied wearily. 'I pulled away some of the connections.'

He crossed to the pipe, and pulled out the rest of the wires. I moved nearer to one of the Daleks. The moaning was dying down now and the Thals were watching silently. Kristas still had his canister in his huge hands ready to put down any resistance but I think we all guessed that something was happening to the creatures.

The Dalek I was near moved its eye-stick towards me slowly. Its other two sticks were now pointing straight down towards the floor.

'Stop… our power… from failing,' it grated out weakly. The Doctor came over and stood at my shoulder, listening intently.

'Power is our life,' it went on. The voice was getting quieter and quieter now.

'Even if I wanted to,' said the Doctor, 'I don't know how.'

'Then this… is the end… of the Daleks,' the voice said and the last word was almost swallowed away. The eye-stick dropped limply and pointed downwards. I looked around the room. All the machines were the same. Lifeless.

There was quite a long silence and no one moved. Then the Doctor put his hand on the top of the Dalek and gave it a little push. It moved about three inches and stopped.

'They're dead. They're all dead,' I heard Susan whisper.

The Doctor crossed the room, picking his way through the debris carefully. He bent over the Dalek I had destroyed in its glass casing and, with an expression of distaste, removed a slender little chain from round its neck. He came back to where I was standing and held up the chain, and on the end of it I saw the fluid link.

'All safe now, Chesterton, eh?'

Our eyes met. I didn't say a word. There didn't seem to be any point in raking over old ashes.

'Well, you don't bear grudges, young man, do you?' He glanced around the room. 'Plenty of mercury in here, anyway. Incidentally, that Dalek over there, the one you destroyed. Did you notice it had a wire attached to one of its legs? My guess is that electricity wasn't just used to power the casing they wore or fire their guns. I think they needed power to help their hearts beat.'

'I sent Alydon and Ganatus down to destroy their electric plant.'

'Best thing you could have done, my dear fellow,' he replied gravely. 'The best thing among a whole series of brave acts.'

Alydon and a group of about twenty Thals entered the room and they all began to wander about, questioning those that had been in the fight and listening with rapt attention to a dozen different versions. Alydon came over and joined us, after bending over Barbara and Susan who were comforting Ganatus and binding his shoulder with a remnant of material that Kristas ripped off his own tunic.

154

'Are they really dead, Doctor?' Alydon said.

'Yes, the power of the Daleks is finished. This is your planet now, Alydon. You have all the inventions of the Daleks to help you rebuild it.'

Alydon looked around the room in bewilderment.

'I don't know how any of these things work.'

'Then you have things to learn,' remarked the Doctor.

'If only we could have achieved our learning without so much sacrifice.'

The Doctor regarded him seriously.

'Don't waste the lives that some of your people have given. If you say to me, "Why should we ever make war again?" then now I not only agree with you, I insist that you follow your principles.'

I said, 'But remember also, Alydon, that you must go on fighting. You must battle with the soil and the sun, fight the creatures in the lake and struggle to keep life itself an ever-increasing thing of beauty.'

'And, if I may have the last word, Chesterton,' put in the Doctor quietly, 'always search for the truth.' He looked away from Alydon and weighed the fluid link in his hand. 'Be straightforward,' he went on. 'It's surprising how much trouble can come from a small deception.'

Barbara didn't say a word to me on the journey back to the forest and although there was a triumphant feast that night she kept well away from me. She sat between the injured Ganatus and Alydon. From time to time, I sensed that she was looking at me but she always averted her eyes whenever I looked at her.

At the end of the evening, as we sat within a ring of the fire-boxes, the Thals rained gifts on us and embarrassed us all with compliments. Embarrassed us all that is, except the

Doctor, who accepted every present and every fine word with a grandness that somehow managed to avoid superiority or any sense of being patronizing. He was absolutely in his element and rose, as I guessed he would, to make a short speech to close the evening celebrations.

'My friends,' he began, and one thumb securely hooked itself in his waistcoat pocket while his other hand hung at his side ready for a battery of theatrical gestures. 'My friends, we have shared an adventure with you. Together we have faced the power of the Daleks and won a magnificent victory. You can be sure we didn't leave the city without searching every nook and cranny and everywhere the story was the same. The Daleks were all dead. That dreadful evil has been wiped away and all that's good can prosper. As for us, my granddaughter, my two friends and I, we must leave you.'

'Stay with us,' a dozen voices chorused but he shook his head sadly.

'Our way is through the stars, my friends. One day perhaps I may come back and visit your grandchildren and see how they have succeeded. There will be birds on this planet then and beautiful flowers. Culture and grace will thrive and this adventure will be a legend.' He gazed around him impressively and held up one finger.

'See that that legend,' he said gravely, 'is the lowest rung on a ladder to happiness, peace and success.'

He sat down to a burst of applause and cheering and looked across at me.

'Chesterton, we might slip away now, I think.'

I nodded and looked round for Barbara, but her place was empty.

People were beginning to get up from the ground and stretch themselves and the women started to collect up the remnants of the feast and put things in order. The Doctor touched my arm.

'The last thing we want to do,' he murmured, 'is prolong the good-byes. I hate sentiment but I have a feeling these people can arouse it in me.' He polished his glasses vigorously on his sleeve and adjusted them on his nose.

'Come along now,' he said almost roughly.

We drifted away from the Thals and made for the *Tardis*. Susan was there already with the doors wide open. I could see behind her through the white light and still found the immenseness of the interior a baffling thing against the cramped look of the police-box exterior,

Susan said, 'Isn't Barbara with you?'

'I'll go and search her out,' I suggested. The Doctor agreed and told me not to be too long.

'We must have a talk,' he said mysteriously then followed Susan back into the Ship.

I went back to the glade where the feast had been set and asked Dyoni if she'd seen Barbara but without success. Then Alydon gave me a clue.

'You should find Kristas,' he remarked. I suppose I must have frowned a bit because he clapped me on the shoulder and his eyes screwed up with laughter.

'You asked him to watch over her, I understand. He's a very simple, straightforward fellow. You haven't released him from the order yet and I believe he'd fight a million Daleks if you asked him to.'

I walked through the forest in the direction Alydon said he had last seen Kristas. It was a well-beaten path and my feet disturbed nothing as I walked. They were sitting together on a dead tree that had fallen on its side and a fire-box gleamed brightly at the giant's feet. I stopped where I was in the shadow of a huge bush, fearful to touch it in case it crackled and powdered and gave me away.

'Can't I tell Ian?' Kristas was saying.

'No! Oh, I don't know. Kristas, what am I going to say to him?'

There was a silence.

Barbara went on. 'He hates me. I know he does. I was stupid. Trying to fight… the way I felt.'

I wonder neither of them could hear my heart pounding. Was I hearing things properly? There was another long silence and I hardly dared to breathe.

'I don't know about these things,' said Kristas slowly, 'but I know that time is never wasted, Barbara. You and he have been forced together, a bond has been created. Let time test both your feelings.' He picked up a branch and began snapping little pieces off it and throwing them away. 'Mind you, I'm speaking from my knowledge, my little knowledge,' he added with a smile, 'of you as a person. My own ways are simple and direct. There was a girl I sat next to at the feast tonight. Salthyana was her name. I will tell her tomorrow that I wish her to stay at my side for the rest of our lives, but that,' he ended seriously, 'would be too direct for you I suppose?'

Barbara said 'Yes,' very softly and added, 'Besides, the man asks the woman if she is willing.'

Then she got to her feet.

'I'm going back to find the Doctor and Susan now. Otherwise, they'll come looking for me.'

I thought she would see me. I could have put out a hand and touched her shoulder but her eyes were busy on the ground and she walked by without noticing. Kristas threw down his stick and rubbed his hands together, then he bent down and started to pick up the five-box. I waited until Barbara was out of earshot then moved from the shadow of the bush. Kristas gave a muffled exclamation but smiled when he saw who it was.

158

'Then you know?'

I held out my hand to him. He put down the fire-box, and grasped it.

'We're going with the Doctor now. He's asked me not to say any good-byes, but I couldn't leave without a word to you. You've been my friend, Kristas, and I'll never forget you.'

Whatever sadness I saw in his eyes must have been in mine as well. Our hands gripped together and I had the greatest difficulty in not wincing with pain.

'Good-bye, Ian. I wish you wouldn't go but I see your way is set.'

I felt a ridiculous prickling in my eyes so I turned quickly and walked away from him, through that dead forest for the last time, my footsteps hurrying to take me away and leading me faster and faster towards the Ship. Just as I reached the glade, I saw Alydon and Dyoni in the distance. His arm was around her shoulders and her face was turned up towards his. There was a look on it of such intense happiness that I strangled the few words I wanted to say and walked quietly through the doors of the Ship, content with the memories I took with me.

CHAPTER TEN

A New Life

I saw Susan press a switch and the doors closed behind me. The Doctor turned and leaned his hands behind him on the control panel. Barbara had her back half turned to me.

'Ah, yes,' said the Doctor, in a business-like way, 'we've been waiting for you, young man.'

I crossed the control room and sat down in the arm-chair.

'Chesterton,' he muttered, 'and Miss Wright.' She turned and faced him and then sat down on a low stool near the Ormulu clock. Susan folded her arms and looked from one to the other of us.

'I can't promise either of you to return you to your planet Earth. I have said that before and I repeat it now. The *Tardis*, although excellent in many respects, does have one or two faults in it. I can never, for example, plan a journey with any accuracy. Both of you, if I may say so, have carried yourselves very well. Intruders you started out but it has been as friends and companions that I recognize your values.'

He left his place by the control column and walked over to the double doors.

'Now, outside these doors,' he said, turning, 'we know there is a world and a very interesting one. The people are delightful and there is much to do. It would be a very full life and a very satisfying one. To build a planet, Chesterton, now there's a challenge for you.'

I inclined my head in agreement.

'Less than a hundred people to populate it and tame it. You

would be assured of good positions in such a society.'

Barbara said, 'You make it sound very attractive.'

'I mean to,' he said. 'For what can I offer you? Constant danger. No permanence. A life of drifting from place to place, searching perhaps for the ideal and never finding it. Mind you,

if you wish to stay with us, Susan and I agree we would be glad of your company. If, on the other hand, one or both of you prefer to stay…'

'Then we shall be dreadfully sorry,' finished Susan for him and he nodded agreement with a sharp move of the head.

There was a short silence while Barbara and I looked at each other. I thought there was a tiny smile on her lips. I know there was one on mine.

'I'll let Barbara decide for both of us,' I said. The Doctor frowned.

'Why?'

'Because the man,' I murmured, 'always asks the woman if she is willing.'

I saw something move in her eyes and a faint blush tinged her cheeks. The light made her eyes glisten and I knew she was remembering everything she'd told Kristas in the wood and knowing I must have overheard it. The Doctor looked at her briefly then directed his gaze at me. It was not at all unkindly.

'It seems to me,' he said gently, 'that the young lady hasn't made up her mind.'

I waited.

Barbara said, 'Can we stay with the Doctor, Ian?'

I saw Susan and her grandfather smile at each other. I got up and walked over to Barbara and took her hand lightly. I felt her fingers pressing into mine. Asking for comfort? Affection? I still didn't dare hope it might be love. Only time could tell. I turned and faced the Doctor with a smile.

'We stay with you,' I said.

About the authors

David Whitaker

Born in April 1928, David Whitaker started his career in the theatre – writing, acting and directing – and was commissioned to adapt one of his plays for television. He was subsequently invited to join the Script Department at the BBC, writing scripts for plays, comedy, and series.

Whitaker's enthusiasm for *Doctor Who* was immense. As the first Story Editor (a position later called Script Editor) he was responsible for finding and commissioning writers then working with them to deliver final scripts. It was Whitaker as much as anyone who defined the narrative 'shape' of *Doctor Who*.

In addition to this work, Whitaker wrote for the *Doctor Who* annuals, novelised the first Dalek story and his own script of *The Crusade*, and worked with Terry Nation on various Dalek-related material including the hugely successful comic strip *The Daleks* which appeared in the Gerry Anderson magazine *TV Century 21*.

Whitaker's own scripts for the programme, in particular his two Dalek stories for the Second Doctor – *The Power of the Daleks* and *The Evil of the Daleks* – are remembered as being amongst the very best of *Doctor Who*.

David Whitaker died in February 1980.

Terry Nation

Terry Nation was born in August 1930 in Llandaff in South Wales. Nation started as a comedy writer and performer, although much of his later drama writing was influenced by his memories of growing up during the Second World War – as he pointed out, the Daleks are based very much on Nazis.

He quickly realised that he was better at writing than performing, however, and went on to provide material for various comedians, including Frankie Howerd, during the 1950s.

In 1962, Nation scripted three episodes of ABC's *Out of this World* science fiction anthology series. Two were adapted from short stories, but the third was an original work called *Botany Bay*. From this he moved on to write an episode of the series *No Hiding Place*.

While working with comedian Tony Hancock, Nation was approached with an offer to work on *Doctor Who*. He was not initially impressed with the format of the series, but after a falling out with Hancock found himself without work. So he quickly accepted the *Doctor Who* job, hurriedly providing the seven episodes of the first ever Dalek story before moving on to further work.

After inventing the Daleks, Nation went on to work on several prestigious ITC television series including *The Saint*, *The Baron* (on which he was Script Supervisor), *The Champions*, *The Avengers* (where he became Script Editor), *Department S*, *The Persuaders!* (as Associate Producer and Story Consultant), and the Gerry Anderson-produced series *The Protectors*.

In the 1970s, Nation was once again working for the BBC. He provided a play starring Robert Hardy as *The Incredible Robert Baldick* which was intended by Nation to be the pilot for a series. Following this he scripted four more Dalek series for *Doctor Who* – including 'Genesis of the Daleks', which has been voted the best ever story in the series.

Also in the mid 1970s, Nation created the popular series *Survivors* which depicted the survivors of a Britain in a world all but wiped out by plague and struggling to cling on to civilisation. The series was revived and updated by the BBC in 2008. In the late 1970s, Nation also devised the hugely popular BBC science fiction series *Blake's 7*.

Terry Nation and his family moved to Los Angeles in 1980, where he continued to work in television providing scripts and ideas. It was in Los Angeles that Terry Nation died, in March 1997.

Doctor Who and the Daleks
Between the Lines

Doctor Who in an exciting adventure with the Daleks by David Whitaker was first published in hardback by Frederick Muller Ltd on 12 November 1964. *Doctor Who*'s second season had begun transmission on BBC television almost three weeks earlier, and it was just nine days before the Daleks' second television adventure – 'The Dalek Invasion of Earth' – was broadcast. The novelisation featured internal illustrations (used in this edition) and a cover by Arnold Schwartzman; almost a year later, on 4 October 1965, it was reprinted by Armada Paperbacks with a new cover and inside illustrations by Peter Archer. It would later be one of the three reprinted titles that launched Universal-Tandem's range of *Doctor Who* books under the Target imprint on 2 May 1973, this time as *Doctor Who and the Daleks*, and with Arnold Schwartzman's illustrations reinstated.

This new edition re-presents that 1973 version. While a few minor errors or inconsistencies have been corrected, no attempt has been made to update or modernise the text – this is *Doctor Who and the Daleks* as originally written and published.

This means that the novel retains certain stylistic and editorial practices that were current in 1964 but which have since adapted or changed, including paragraphing conventions that are quite different from current usage.

Most obviously, all measurements are given in the then-standard imperial system of weights and measures: a yard is equivalent to 0.9144 metres; three feet make a yard, and a foot is 30 centimetres; twelve inches make a foot, and an inch is

25.4 millimetres. The Thal Alydon is described as 'six foot four', meaning six feet and four inches (1.93 metres).

In common with the television scripts at the time, the name of the Doctor's time machine is given here as '*Tardis*' or 'the *Tardis*'; only in the 1970s did the series' 'house style' establish 'TARDIS' as the standard usage, still used in 2011. (Susan, on television and in print, credits herself with making up the name from the initials of 'Time And Relative Dimension In Space', though this novel actually features the first appearance of the plural 'Dimensions' that was subsequently used on TV for many years.) As on television, and in almost every novel, the Doctor himself is 'the Doctor' and never 'Doctor Who' or 'Dr Who'; 1963's TV dialogue 'Eh? Doctor who? What's he talking about?' and 'Who is he? Doctor who? Perhaps if we knew his name we might have a clue to all this' become, in this print version, Ian's suggestion: 'Perhaps that's what we ought to call him – "Doctor Who"?' Susan, meanwhile – known as 'Susan Foreman' on television, after the name painted on the junkyard gates – is here given the surname 'English', presumably chosen to be nicely inconspicuous.

The Doctor is said to be 'very rich', paying Barbara £20 per week for Susan's tuition (more than £300 at 2011 prices). Jon Pertwee's Third Doctor stated in 1970 that he had 'no use for the stuff', an attitude that has remained part of the Doctor's character ever since, but money was rarely mentioned in 1960s *Doctor Who*. Whitaker does, though, use a couple of pre-decimal coins for comparisons, first to the size of a half-crown (a 32-millimetre coin, valued at two shillings and sixpence – a little under £2 in today's money); the second to the size of shillings (24-millimetre coins, replaced in the early 1970s with the 5p denomination, and now equivalent to about 77p). The Doctor is also depicted as having a 'gold hunter on a thick chain', a vintage pocket watch.

The Dalek city is described as resembling the work of the American architect Frank Lloyd Wright, who had died in 1959 and was famous for his 'organic architecture', designed to integrate buildings with their surroundings. In Chapter Six, Ian feels he knows 'how men in the Tank Corps suffered when an enemy bazooka suddenly appeared', a reference to a unit of the British Army established during the First World War that was officially replaced by the Royal Tank Regiment in 1939. He also refers to the four travellers proceeding in 'Indian file fashion', a reference to Native Americans that simply means 'single file'.

While *Doctor Who in an exciting adventure with the Daleks* would eventually spearhead a range of more than 150 novelisations (and, later, inspire more than 300 original novels), in 1964 it was effectively a one-off. It was adapted from *Doctor Who*'s second television adventure, 'The Daleks', which prompted David Whitaker to devise the entirely new introduction to the four main characters seen in the first couple of chapters. The after-school encounter in a London junkyard and a three-part ordeal in Earth's Stone Age are exchanged for a car crash and a meeting on Barnes Common. The tone of the novel at this point is also rather different from the television series, with Ian Chesterton's first-person narration giving us fairly graphic descriptions of a fatal road accident, making the Doctor an even more mysterious and untrustworthy character than he'd seemed on TV, and showing Ian himself smoking cigarettes. (That's a sign of the times – smoking was a much more widespread habit in the 1960s than it is now, and the Doctor himself had lit up a pipe, for the first and last time, in the second television episode. Ian's novelised experiences on Skaro seem to have kicked the habit for him, too. Nowadays, Alydon's cloak would probably be compared to tracing rather than cigarette paper.)

The structure of this new first encounter with the Doctor is quite similar to the events of the first television episode, 'An Unearthly Child', keeping all the main story 'beats' in place and reprising or echoing some of that episode's dialogue. Ian's criticism of Barbara for letting things out 'a bit at a time' recalls his observation in 'An Unearthly Child' that Susan 'lets her knowledge out a bit at a time so as not to embarrass me', and the Doctor is here given the same first line as he'd had on television in that junkyard – 'What are you doing here?' Barbara, too, has dialogue in the novel derived from televised exchanges, like her determination 'to have a chat with this grandfather of hers'.

The conclusion of this account is the same: Ian and Barbara force their way into the TARDIS, and the Doctor impulsively spirits them away to a life of adventure in time and space. The TARDIS control room is, as on TV, dotted with antique chairs and bric-a-brac, some identified in this novel as a Chippendale, a Sheraton and an Ormulu clock – these examples of eighteenth-century furniture, together with the bust of Napoleon, tie in with Susan's televised observation that the French Revolution (1789–1799) is the Doctor's favourite period of Earth history. So, too, does Susan's thirty-page essay on Robespierre, itself a development from a scene in 'An Unearthly Child' where she leafs through a thick volume on the French Revolution and comments, 'That's not right.' The list of the gaps and errors in her knowledge is wholly new, but again fits in with her not understanding the details of contemporary British currency in the first episode.

The Doctor's description of the delights of exploring time and space is also reminiscent of dialogue from the earliest television episodes: 'It's … a privilege to step out on to new soil and see an alien sun wheeling above you in another sky' recalls his transmitted line 'If you could touch the alien sand and hear the cries of strange birds, and watch them wheel in another sky... would that satisfy you?'

The first-person narrative is from Ian Chesterton's viewpoint, but Whitaker strengthens the characterisation of the Doctor considerably, emphasising his keen intelligence over the more obvious signs of ageing portrayed by William Hartnell. The Doctor even takes some of Ian's televised lines, such as when he quickly deduces that Susan may have placed the Thals in danger ('This Alydon of yours seems to have kept his wits about him').

Whitaker also took the opportunity to expand our knowledge of the Doctor's time machine. In addition to the food machine seen on screen, the TARDIS is now equipped with a highly advanced shower and shaver that Ian uses, though they're never seen on screen. (Ian says the haircut he gets in the TARDIS is as good as one from Simpson's of Piccadilly, a Central London department store that traded between 1936 and 1999.) Ian is also assigned a bedroom – on television, the question was slightly fudged, but there seemed to be a communal sleeping area. The circular indentations adorning the TARDIS walls – much later identified as 'roundels' – can be opened and used as storage space, something that would not be true on television for twenty years. There's still a 'yearometer' which 'was damaged on a previous expedition'; on TV, it stopped working as soon as the TARDIS left 1963 London. Missing from the novel is the faulty radiation meter that fails to warn them of Skaro's dangers in 'The Daleks'; instead, the Doctor is provoked into leading them from the ship prematurely, despite Susan's warnings that they've not checked everything properly. When they exit the ship on Skaro, it is still disguised as a police box, and there's no explanation here of the TARDIS's theoretical ability to disguise itself.

Ian's initial disbelief and Barbara's more open-minded response to what the Doctor and Susan tell them mirrors their attitudes on screen. The Doctor remains supercilious, although Whitaker here has him deciding that Susan needs a twentieth-century education, rather than 'that ridiculous school' being Susan's choice in 'An Unearthly Child'. His uncertainty over how far human science has progressed ('you've discovered television, haven't you?') is echoed here when Susan breaks in to correct 'aeronautical machine' to 'aeroplane'. He and Susan are 'cut off from our own planet', the same phrase as used in the first episode, though Whitaker adds here that they are 'separated from it by a million, million years of your time'. *Doctor Who*'s writers have always liked big numbers. And, like a lot of the television scripts of the time, the word 'universe' tends to be used interchangeably with 'solar system' and 'galaxy' ('Forget about your planet. We're already in the next Universe but one').

Once the TARDIS arrives on Skaro, the novel's plot follows that of the television original very closely, although a number of televised scenes that don't involve Ian directly are omitted. The putative romance between Ian and Barbara means that Barbara's onscreen closeness with the Thal Ganatus is entirely dispensed with. Other variations include Ian easily escaping his Dalek casing disguise, where the third episode of 'The Daleks' gains several minutes of tension from him being trapped inside it with hostile Daleks just moments away. The neutron war is said to have taken place 200 years before the events of the novel; this was 'over 500 years ago' on screen. Whitaker's novel originally described the Dalek machines as about three feet tall and then as about four foot six inches; this has been corrected to five feet (about 1.52 metres). The Doctor theorises that the Dalek creatures' mutation is not complete, and the TV episodes suggest that the Thals have fully mutated to become more or less perfect; in 1975, however, 'Genesis of the Daleks' informs us that the Dalek's creator, Davros, has conducted experiments to discover his people's final mutated form and then invented travel machines for them – the Daleks.

Whitaker also devises an extra element to Ian's efforts to convince the Thals to fight, the boxing match described in Chapter Seven, and the death of Antodus is revised to have him stumble on a creeper after successfully jumping the chasm, rather than the failed jump seen on TV. And the final chapter features an entirely new sequence in which the Doctor offers Ian and Barbara a place aboard the TARDIS, which they accept. On the small screen, *Doctor Who*'s first two seasons centred on the Doctor's continuing attempt to pilot the TARDIS to return the pair home to 1960s Earth.

On publication in 1964, the novel also provided a few glimpses of *Doctor Who*'s future. Susan's observation that she'd have worried about her grandfather had she stayed the night at Barbara's flat quietly foreshadows her exchange with the Doctor when she leaves the TARDIS to settle on Earth after the Dalek invasion, in an episode broadcast a few weeks after this novel's publication. So does Ian's musing on whether the Doctor and Susan 'understand such Earth-like customs as marriage' and what will happen when the granddaughter decides to leave her grandfather. The title of the fourth chapter, 'The Power of the Daleks', was later used by Whitaker when he scripted Patrick Troughton's first adventure as the Second Doctor. Chapter Nine introduces the Daleks' leader, another Dalek mutant, which sits inside a glass casing. In 1960s comic strips featuring the Daleks, their leader was the Emperor, who subsequently appeared in 'The Evil of the Daleks' in 1967, though not in a glass casing and with a deep and resonant voice rather than 'a dreadful squeaking sound'. But a glass Dalek did eventually appear on television, in 1985's 'Revelation of the Daleks'.

Most significant, perhaps, is the frequent appearance of a certain word. In their first few television stories, the Daleks 'fire', 'destroy' and 'annihilate'; it's not until David Whitaker's pair of Dalek scripts for Patrick Troughton's Doctor in 1966/7 that the Daleks really develop their famous catchphrase. *Doctor Who and the Daleks* can lay claim to the first regular use of the Daleks' battle-cry: 'Exterminate!'

Here are details of other exciting Doctor Who *titles from BBC Books:*

DOCTOR WHO AND THE CRUSADERS
David Whitaker   £4.99
ISBN 978 1 849 90190 1   **A First Doctor adventure**

With a new introduction by **CHARLIE HIGSON**

'I admire bravery, sir. And bravery and courage are clearly in you in full measure. Unfortunately, you have no brains at all. I despise fools.'

Arriving in the Holy Land in the middle of the Third Crusade, the Doctor and his companions run straight into trouble. The Doctor and Vicki befriend Richard the Lionheart, but must survive the cut-throat politics of the English court. Even with the king on their side, they find they have made powerful enemies.

Looking for Barbara, Ian is ambushed – staked out in the sand and daubed with honey so that the ants will eat him. With Ian unable to help, Barbara is captured by the cruel warlord El Akir. Even if Ian escapes and rescues her, will they ever see the Doctor, Vicki and the TARDIS again?

This novel is based on a Doctor Who *story which was originally broadcast from 27 March to 17 April 1965, featuring the First Doctor as played by William Hartnell, and his companions Ian, Barbara and Vicki.*

DOCTOR WHO AND THE CYBERMEN
Gerry Davis £4.99
ISBN 978 1 849 90191 8 **A Second Doctor adventure**

With a new introduction by **GARETH ROBERTS**

'There are some corners of the universe which have bred the most terrible things. Things which are against everything we have ever believed in. They must be fought. To the death.'

In 2070, the Earth's weather is controlled from a base on the moon. But when the Doctor and his friends arrive, all is not well. They discover unexplained drops of air pressure, minor problems with the weather control systems, and an outbreak of a mysterious plague.

With Jamie injured, and members of the crew going missing, the Doctor realises that the moonbase is under attack. Some malevolent force is infecting the crew and sabotaging the systems as a prelude to an invasion of Earth. And the Doctor thinks he knows who is behind it: the Cybermen.

This novel is based on 'The Moonbase', a Doctor Who *story which was originally broadcast from 11 February to 4 March 1967, featuring the Second Doctor as played by Patrick Troughton, and his companions Polly, Ben and Jamie.*

DOCTOR WHO AND THE ABOMINABLE SNOWMEN
Terrance Dicks   £4.99
ISBN 978 1 849 90192 5   **A Second Doctor adventure**

With a new introduction by **STEPHEN BAXTER**

'Light flooded into the tunnel, silhouetting the enormous shaggy figure in the cave mouth. With a blood-curdling roar, claws outstretched, it bore down on Jamie.'

The Doctor has been to Det-Sen Monastery before, and expects the welcome of a lifetime. But the monastery is a very different place from when the Doctor last came. Fearing an attack at any moment by the legendary Yeti, the monks are prepared to defend themselves, and see the Doctor as a threat.

The Doctor and his friends join forces with Travers, an English explorer out to prove the existence of the elusive abominable snowmen. But they soon discover that these Yeti are not the timid animals that Travers seeks. They are the unstoppable servants of an alien Intelligence.

This novel is based on a Doctor Who *story which was originally broadcast from 30 September to 4 November 1967, featuring the Second Doctor as played by Patrick Troughton, and his companions Jamie and Victoria.*

DOCTOR WHO AND THE AUTON INVASION

Terrance Dicks £4.99

ISBN 978 1 849 90193 2 A Third Doctor adventure

With a new introduction by RUSSELL T DAVIES

'Here at UNIT we deal with the odd – the unexplained. We're prepared to tackle anything on Earth. Or even from beyond the Earth, if necessary.'

Put on trial by the Time Lords, and found guilty of interfering in the affairs of other worlds, the Doctor is exiled to Earth in the 20th century, his appearance once again changed. His arrival coincides with a meteorite shower. But these are no ordinary meteorites.

The Nestene Consciousness has begun its first attempt to invade Earth using killer Autons and deadly shop window dummies. Only the Doctor and UNIT can stop the attack. But the Doctor is recovering in hospital, and his old friend the Brigadier doesn't even recognise him. Can the Doctor recover and win UNIT's trust before the invasion begins?

This novel is based on 'Spearhead from Space', a Doctor Who *story which was originally broadcast from 3 to 24 January 1970, featuring the Third Doctor as played by Jon Pertwee, with his companion Liz Shaw and the UNIT organisation commanded by Brigadier Lethbridge-Stewart.*

DOCTOR WHO AND THE CAVE MONSTERS
Malcolm Hulke £4.99
ISBN 978 1 849 90194 9 **A Third Doctor adventure**

With a new introduction by **TERRANCE DICKS**

'Okdel looked across the valley to see the tip of the sun as it sank below the horizon. It was the last time he was to see the sun for a hundred million years.'

UNIT are called in to investigate security at a secret research centre buried under Wenley Moor. Unknown to the Doctor and his colleagues, the work at the centre has woken a group of Silurians – intelligent reptiles that used to be the dominant life form on Earth in prehistoric times.

Now they have woken, the Silurians are appalled to find 'their' planet populated by upstart apes. The Doctor hopes to negotiate a peace deal, but there are those on both sides who cannot bear the thought of humans and Silurians living together. As UNIT soldiers enter the cave systems, and the Silurians unleash a deadly plague that could wipe out the human race, the battle for planet Earth begins.

This novel is based on 'The Silurians', a Doctor Who *story which was originally broadcast from 31 January to 14 March 1970, featuring the Third Doctor as played by Jon Pertwee, with his companion Liz Shaw and the UNIT organisation commanded by Brigadier Lethbridge-Stewart.*